ONLY EVER US

Light My Fire Series

J.H. CROIX

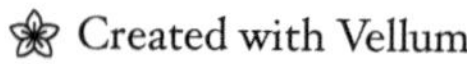 Created with Vellum

To one of my favorite people in the universe, LM. You were grace & kindness personified with a healthy dose of hilarity thrown in. I'll always remember you when I laugh.

Sign up for my newsletter for information on new releases & get a FREE copy of one of my books!

http://jhcroixauthor.com/subscribe/

Follow me!
jhcroix@jhcroix.com
https://amazon.com/author/jhcroix
https://www.bookbub.com/authors/j-h-croix
https://www.facebook.com/jhcroix
https://www.instagram.com/jhcroix/

Chapter One

MAE

I glanced around the small room, where the smoothly polite pastor's assistant had deposited me. The only window offered a misty view. The drizzle falling outside earlier had ended, leaving an almost otherworldly glittering landscape with the sun breaking through the clouds. My throat was tight, and my chest ached. She was gone. And, somehow, I had to get through this.

I took a breath, trying to ease the tightness in my chest, and blinked against the sting of tears in my eyes. My eyes dipped down to the notebook my grandmother had left behind. I finally lifted it and flipped it open, a laugh bubbling up only seconds later as I read the first sentence.

Stop crying. I've lived a very good life, and you know it. Now, get your act together. Wipe those tears and do this right. I don't want a big funeral, for God's sake. My chest loosened. *I'm not going to say anything ridiculous, and I promise I won't haunt anyone. Who has time for that? I always loved you, and maybe you're fed up with my opinions. Lord knows I have plenty. I'm still somewhere. Take care of yourself and go kick life's butt.*

I lowered the notebook, letting it fall closed as another chuckle slipped out. I finally took the deepest breath I'd been able to take in months. Gram *had* lived a good life, and she'd lived it on her terms. I'd been meaning to come home anyway, so I supposed I was grateful she'd brought me here. Although I was hurting that it was her illness and then death that kicked my ass in gear.

I still remembered our last conversation from a month and a half ago. She'd given me "man advice," her words. The last thing I'd wanted.

There was a soft knock on the door, and I quickly swiped at the tears that had already started to dry on my cheeks. "Yes?" I called.

Margie—I thought that was her name—peered in. "He'll be with you in just a few minutes. You can have a seat if you'd like. We're finishing up another service."

I didn't know what to think about them having a service at the church while I waited to meet with the pastor to plan Gram's funeral. You couldn't schedule death. It might be the only thing you couldn't schedule in life these days. Speaking of scheduling, my parents were running late and had texted to apologize after my father got a flat tire.

After Margie disappeared, I circled the small room, restlessness making me jittery. A table by the door contained a brochure for coffins, along with another one for urns. Death was no barrier to brochures.

Crossing the room, I idly counted the row of candles by the window. A loud humming sound seemed to be coming from the nearby closet. Antsy and bored, I traced my fingertips along the edges of the candleholders.

Turning away, I started flipping through the brochure on urns. I felt like I was walking a tightrope. To one side lay heavy grief and tears. To the other side lay hysteria. At this moment, hysteria bubbled up, and I started laughing. Even urns were marketed with glossy ads.

"Yay for capitalism," I muttered to myself.

I swiped at the next round of tears that slipped down my cheeks just as I heard a whooshing sound. I turned to discover flames flickering along the edges of the closet—the closet right between the door and the only window, the only two exits out of this room.

Like an idiot, I raced directly toward the door in the tiny room. I reached for the doorknob but then snatched my hand away swiftly. It was burning hot to the touch. Flames flickered out of the closet, catching on the curtains by the window. I reached for the door-knob again and leaped back when there was a whooshing sound. The curtains and a sash hanging on a hook by the door had caught fire.

Dear God. This room was filled with fabric things, all of them flammable. I looked around frantically as smoke filled the space. I heard voices in the hallway and dashed toward the window, only to leap back at the blast of heat from the flames.

Fuck. I was supposed to be meeting the pastor for my grandmother's funeral, and now I was in my own pyre. Long moments later—I really had no idea how much time passed—I heard loud footsteps. When the door opened, I saw broad shoulders looming through the thick smoke before strong arms reached for me. I'd pinned myself in the corner, the only spot in this room that seemed safe from the flames as they over-took the entire wall.

"I've got you," a low voice murmured.

Even though the room was on fire, I knew—*knew*—that voice.

I coughed. What were the freaking chances that Rowan Cole would walk in here to rescue me? I wanted to tell him to put me down. But, well, fire.

Of course, Rowan lifted me easily. Even though he was wearing heavy gear, I could feel his muscled arms and chest as he cradled me against him and carried me down the hallway.

The hallway was filled with smoke, and I struggled to get a breath every step of the way. We burst out the back door, and I gulped in the fresh air, coughing again.

"I've got you, Mae," Rowan murmured again.

I was annoyed that he even knew it was me.

"Put me down," I demanded between hacking coughs.

"Nope."

If I didn't know better, I would've thought he might be amused by my predicament. He carried me straight over to an emergency vehicle parked near my car. I heard voices exclaiming around me.

"I don't even know what happened!"

"How did the room catch on fire?"

I couldn't even differentiate the voices. Rowan ignored everyone and lowered me carefully onto a stretcher beside the emergency vehicle. "She probably needs some oxygen," he said to the woman waiting there.

"I'm fine," I insisted, coughing again to disprove my own point.

I looked up into Rowan's face. Despite the fact I'd

just been carried out of a burning room, my belly managed to do a little shimmy and a twist at the sight of him up close. Ugh. I was annoyed that he was my rescuer, yet apparently, my hormones thought he was *all* that.

"I'm fine," I repeated. I managed not to cough this time, though my throat hurt and my voice was raspy.

"Surrender to the process, Mae. You need oxygen." Rowan's green eyes looked concerned as they coasted over me. He reached for the hand I'd used to open the door and turned it over. "She needs something on that palm, Dana."

I looked toward the woman, opening my mouth to protest. I finally got a look at her and recognized Dana Halloran from high school. I hadn't seen her since I'd moved back to town.

Before I could get a word out, she held up an oxygen mask and placed it over my mouth. "You need oxygen. I'll look at your hand next." Dana glanced at Rowan. "You need to help fight that fire," she offered pointedly.

I started to laugh and coughed instead. Rowan muttered something I couldn't hear and turned, striding away quickly. I took several deep breaths, actually relieved to breathe. Pure oxygen was pretty cool stuff, especially when you needed it. After a few moments, the tight, prickly feeling in my lungs eased, and I began to relax. Dana was still waiting beside me.

She lowered the mask from my face. "Better?"

I took a deep breath, savoring the cool air. "I think so."

Dana was pretty in a practical sort of way. Her curly hair was pulled back in a ponytail, and she had big brown eyes. "Now, let me look at that hand." After she set down the oxygen mask, she turned my palm over. "That's a minor burn. Let me put some cream on it."

The edges of my palm were an angry red, and it stung. "I'm sure it's fine," I lied.

"I promise this will make it feel better." She opened up a small cloth bag on the stretcher. She smoothed some cream over the reddened areas, and it did feel better. "You know Rowan?" She looked back up at me.

I twisted my lips to the side. "Yes, we went to college together."

"Really?" Her brows lifted in surprise.

"I went to college in North Carolina."

"Ah, that's right. He's from there, just like Remy. Wow. Small world."

The world was feeling more than a little *too* small these days with Rowan here in Alaska.

"What's that look for?" Dana pressed as she set my hand down.

"Thank you, that actually does feel better."

"That's what it's supposed to do," she offered with a quick smile. "You happen to have some history with Rowan?"

I rolled my eyes. "Nothing important. I'll have to thank him for rescuing me." I wasn't about to go into my history with Rowan with Dana or anyone else for that matter.

She shrugged. "I don't think you need to thank him. It's his job. Literally."

Chapter Two

ROWAN

Once the fire was under control, I returned to check on Mae. While I was waiting, Carrie Dodge, an elderly woman whose cat I had rescued just last week, came walking over.

"Mae!" she exclaimed. "What in the world happened?"

"Hey, Aunt Carrie. The closet caught fire and then the curtains, I think." Mae tried to take a deep breath and only coughed again. Dana slapped the oxygen mask back over her mouth.

Carrie looked up at me. "That's my great-niece," she announced.

I looked over at Mae, and her eyes met mine from just above the oxygen mask on her face. She stayed silent. Even coughing, distressed, and just carted out of a fire, Mae was still beautiful. Her blond hair fell in a tangle around her shoulders, and her ginger eyes were snapping.

"How are you, honey?" Carrie asked as she stepped closer to Mae and patted her on the shoulder.

Mae blinked at her. Dana interjected, "Give her a

minute. With a little more oxygen, she probably won't need to cough again."

Carrie turned her attention back to me. "Thank you."

"For?"

"Rescuing Mae."

"It's my job." When my eyes bounced over to Mae again, hers were narrowed. If eyes could shoot flames, I was certain hers would.

I had tons of questions, but now wasn't the time for any of them. I turned my attention back to the fire. I'd tagged along with the town crew today just because I could. They were at half capacity since part of the crew was out training. As much as I wanted to stand by Mae's side and wait to finally have a freaking conversation with her, now really wasn't the time.

I walked toward the fire truck and stopped beside Susannah, another firefighter. "All taken care of," I commented.

She looked up at me, her lips quirking at the corners in a faint smile. "It was contained in that one room, thank goodness. This is the only funeral place in town. I'm just glad it wasn't the church portion of this structure."

The funeral home was attached to the back of the only church in this small town. I glanced over at it. The pastor was standing outside at the base of the stairs, talking to some of the parishioners who'd scurried out. "Do we know if the service was over?"

"Yes. Maisie already called and got the scoop and then reported in."

"Do we know what caused the fire?"

"Apparently, the water heater in that closet caught fire, then the curtains. We'll have more time to check on it later. Nobody got hurt, so it's not an emergency."

I glanced over toward Mae. Dana had removed the oxygen mask, and she and Mae were talking with Carrie. I really wanted to go over there, but I didn't.

This was the second time I'd seen Mae in town. The first had been over two months ago, and then she disappeared again. I still couldn't get over the chances of finding her again.

Dragging my eyes away from her, I left. An hour or so later, after I had showered and changed, Maisie Steele called my name as I was walking down the hallway at the station. Glancing over my shoulder, I stopped and turned. "Yeah?"

"You have a visitor." The door at the end of the hallway swung shut behind her.

Curious as to who would stop by the station to see me, I walked up front into the reception area. It was situated between the fire station and the police station, where the single building served as a shared space. Maisie was the central dispatcher, and she was already on the phone at her command center, as she referred to it.

She smiled over at me and gestured toward the chairs by the windows. I looked over to discover Mae sitting there.

"Hey, Mae." I walked over as my heart kicked into an irregular beat. I wouldn't admit it aloud, but simply seeing her again made me nervous.

Her eyes whipped up from where she'd been looking at her phone. She immediately slipped it into her jacket pocket and stood. "Hi."

Her hair was damp and frozen on the ends. It was early November, and we'd already had snow here. I was accustomed to winter, but not this early, and definitely not this cold. Winters in the mountains of North Carolina weren't like those of Alaska. I'd been warned we weren't even to the coldest part yet. I didn't mind. I loved the mountains, and I loved the snow.

"Thank you," Mae said, her ginger eyes blinking up at me.

"For what?"

Her lips pressed in a line, those lips that were just as inviting as they'd once been years ago. They were pink and full and tipped up at the corners.

"For rescuing me from the fire." Her breath came out in a rush.

"It's my job."

"I know, but still." She stuffed her hands in her pockets.

I didn't know how it was possible, but she'd gotten more beautiful, at least to me. Back when we'd been friends and then a little more in college, she'd been stunning to me. She was medium height with curvy hips. She wore jeans with cowboy boots and a fluffy down jacket. Her blond hair spilled around her shoulders in shades of honey, dark ash, and sunshine. She removed one hand from a pocket and brushed her long bangs to the side.

"What are you doing here?" she asked.

"Uh, I work here."

Mae rolled her eyes. "No, I mean here in my hometown in Alaska."

"My friend, Remy, is one of the firefighters here. He told me about the job."

"What?"

I lifted my shoulders in a shrug. "He's a hotshot firefighter. They travel all over. He's married with a baby on the way here, so he's definitely staying. He thought I'd like it here."

"What are the freaking chances of that?" Mae muttered.

I chuckled. "I don't know."

"It's annoying more than weird."

Mae and I met in college. She'd been on a scholarship in college in North Carolina. To this day, I thought about her more than I'd like to admit.

"Did you know this was my hometown?" she asked.

I shifted my shoulders uncomfortably. "Yeah."

Her eyes coasted over my face curiously. "Yeah?"

"Of course, I remembered, Mae. We were best friends before."

"Before?"

"Before we went on a few dates and you stopped talking to me," I said flatly, ignoring the pain that felt like a spear driven through my heart.

Her breath drew in sharply. She glared at me before she spun away, walking swiftly out the door. I moved to follow her. "Mae!" I called when I reached the parking area.

She glanced over her shoulder. "Let it go, Rowan." She climbed into a small blue car and drove away.

I stood there, watching the glow of her taillights disappear. I sighed and walked back into the station. Maisie looked up as I came in. "What did you do to Mae?"

I crossed over, resting my elbows on the counter that encircled her desk. "I wish I knew."

Maisie wrinkled her nose. "I need you to connect the dots for me, please. How do you know Mae? I didn't think you were from here."

"I'm not. I'm from Stolen Hearts Valley in North Carolina, same town as Remy."

"Oh, that's right! He's the one who told you about the job opening here."

"You got it."

"So, about Mae?"

"We met in college. She had a scholarship to UNC." It wasn't that I wanted to avoid this conversation, but it was uncomfortable because I didn't know what I'd done to piss off Mae. She'd been one of my closest friends, and I'd fallen for her. Hard. I'd finally found the nerve to ask her out. A few dates later, she stopped talking to me and avoided me so thoroughly I never found out what happened.

"Do you know Mae well?" Maisie pressed. Maisie basically ran the station, and even though I'd only been here for a few months, I knew she kept her thumb on the pulse of everything going on. "As far as I know, she just moved back. Her grandmother passed away."

"Yeah, she was Carrie Dodge's sister."

Maisie's brows rose. "Yeah, I know. So, Mae seems pissed off with you?"

"Maybe."

"What did you do?" Maisie pressed just as my friend Remy Martin came through the doors.

"What's up?" he asked, stopping beside me.

"Apparently, Rowan was a dumbass in college," Maisie offered helpfully.

Remy glanced at me, his eyes crinkling with a smile. "Really?"

I sighed, straightening as I ran a hand through my hair. "I don't even know what I did."

"Dude, why do you look so upset?"

I gestured toward the parking lot although Mae was long gone. "You remember Mae Townsend?"

Remy looked as if he were rifling through a cabinet in his brain before he nodded slowly. "You were best friends in college. I thought you had it bad for her."

"Yeah. That's the one. This is her hometown, she hates me, and I don't even know why."

Chapter Three

MAE

"Stupid, stupid, stupid. I'm an idiot," I said.

My grandmother's cat blinked up at me before letting out a loud meow. I looked over at her empty food bowl. She was a chatty cat. Aunt Carrie had given her to me just last week after Gram's memorial service, telling me Sassafras was my grandmother's old cat and she would keep me company.

"You probably need some food."

I stood and crossed over to the kitchen, opening a cabinet and fetching a can of food. This cat was spoiled rotten. According to Aunt Carrie, my grandmother had gotten her last summer before she got sick. Or rather, before she knew she was going to die. I spooned the cat food into the bowl, and Sassafras leaped onto the small table by the windows and settled in to eat.

Curling my arms around my waist, I crossed from the kitchen back into the living room, walking over to the window to stare outside. It was only five in the evening, and the sun was already about to slip behind the horizon, its early evening rays silvery and thin. Sunset would come soon. The days were short and the nights long during Alaskan winters.

I let out a sigh before turning and plunking down on the couch. I kicked my feet up on the coffee table and let my eyes travel around the room. I didn't even know if I wanted to stay here, but this house was mine. I owned it free and clear. All I had to do was pay the annual property taxes.

My throat felt suddenly tight, and I swallowed through the thickness. Gram was gone, and that's why I owned this house. I'd just had an argument with my mother this afternoon about staying. She wanted me to stay. If it weren't for the fact that Rowan was here, I would probably say yes. It was a smart move. I had a house and a good job offer. But I had reasons for reconsidering. Reasons being Rowan. Why did he have to be so freaking handsome? He could have at least gotten less delectable in the years since I'd seen him.

Rowan wasn't directly responsible for my bitterness about men. It's just that he was connected to the worst night of my life. My radar for men who weren't assholes seemed to be broken. I thought about the last guy I'd gone on a date with. It had been a disaster. For one, he wouldn't shut up about football. I didn't have anything against football, but I was a basketball fan through and through.

So, anyway, football. Then he kept calling me babe. On our first date. He'd seemed surprised that I had a doctorate. What the actual fuck? In the past decade, more women than men earned advanced degrees every year.

Then I'd kissed him, and he'd stuffed his tongue down my throat—super annoying. I shouldn't have even kissed him. Of course, I knew how Rowan kissed. He was good at it. *Really* good at it, like master level.

Ugh. I let out a groan, leaning my head back. He was here in Willow Brook and bringing up all kinds of memories. Rowan had been my best friend for a while in college. We'd ended up seated together in my very first class. He was just easy to be with, and we'd become fast friends. It had been platonic at first, but it'd been impossible not to notice how hot he was—all rumpled dark curls, intense green eyes, and a drool-worthy body. I'd started to fall for him but promised myself our friendship was more important. Then he asked me out on a date.

I'd been so thrown, he had to ask me twice.

My eyes stung with tears, and I swiped them away with my palm.

Stupid, stupid, stupid. I didn't need to get all caught up in my feelings about him. I sucked in a deep breath, letting it out slowly. My mind started to turn down a path I avoided. It was dark and held the memory of something I'd do anything to erase. If there was one lesson I'd learned, it was that you couldn't change the past.

I stood abruptly, determined not to spend the night thinking about Rowan or why I'd thought I only had one choice all those years ago.

Because it felt lonely to be here in this house by myself, I decided to head out. Holly, my old friend from high school, had texted earlier and asked if I wanted to get together.

I tapped out a text. *You still want to meet tonight?*

Her answer was swift. *Sure thing. I get off from my shift at the hospital in an hour. Do you want to meet at Firehouse or Wildlands or the new pizza place?*

Me: *Let's try the pizza place. I haven't been there yet.*

Holly: *It's good! See you soon!*

Since Rowan had rescued me, I'd run into him four times. And every time, my hormones fired off like a pinball machine. Twice, he tried to talk to me, and twice, I'd managed to gracefully exit the situation.

The university had emailed last week, telling me they were still holding the position for me, but they would open it up again if I didn't commit soon. I didn't want to go back to North Carolina. I'd missed home, and I was feeling stubborn about Rowan. I wasn't going to let him show up in my hometown and take over. This was *my* hometown. I sat down at my desk and pulled out my laptop, quickly pasting in the acceptance I'd written.

This was a tenure track position in the environmental sciences program, and I didn't want to pass it up. My parents were here, I had a house, and this was my town and my friends. I would just have to deal with Rowan, and my hormones would get a clue. I ignored the tiny voice pointing out that maybe Rowan was a massive reminder of the night I'd prefer to forget, but none of it was his fault.

———

My breath misted in the air as I hurried across the parking lot, pushing through the door into Alpenglow Pizza. The restaurant had been here for a few years, but it was new to me. It was on the outer end of Main Street near the hospital. I did want to try the new pizza, but I'd also wanted to limit my chances of encountering Rowan. During the winter months, Wildlands was a favorite hangout for locals. Since I came back to town, I'd been there a few times, and I'd already encountered Rowan there twice.

I paused and glanced around the restaurant. Booths lined the walls, and a counter at the back had a wood-fired oven visible behind it. It smelled delicious in here.

Holly waved at me from a booth in the corner. I waved as I crossed over to her. Before I could get a word out, Holly stood and pulled me into a quick hug. Her brown eyes twinkled as she stepped back and gave my shoulders a squeeze. "It's so good to see you again!"

"You too."

We sat down across from each other, and Holly brushed her blond hair off her shoulders before lifting a glass of water and taking a swallow. As she set her glass down, she pointed at the one beside my elbow. "I ordered water for you, but I didn't know if you wanted anything else to drink."

"Water will do."

"What do you want to get? Everything is good. I was thinking we should split a pizza." She leaned her elbows on the table and turned the opened menu around for me to read it.

"What do you like? Pepperoni still your favorite?" I asked.

Holly's smile was wide. "Hell, yes."

"Let's just get a whole pepperoni then."

"Deal."

I closed the menu and slipped my arms out of my jacket. Holly and I had been pretty close in high school, but it felt like her life had leapfrogged ahead of mine. She was married and pregnant. The server appeared, and we ordered.

As soon as she was gone, Holly leaned back. "So tell me everything."

"Everything? I don't have a ton of news," I replied with a light laugh.

"Have you decided if you're staying?"

"Yes. I have a house and a good job. It was kind of hard to say no." I kicked Rowan out of my thoughts. "Tell me how you're doing. You probably have more going on than me."

Holly's lips curled in a smile. "Maybe, maybe not. I never left Willow Brook. I took the promotion at the hospital, so I'm the supervisor for the nursing department in the ER. Nate and I are married, but you know that."

"And pretty soon, you'll be a mama," I teased lightly with a glance at her round belly.

Holly's cheeks went a little pink. "Not soon enough. Pregnancy makes me tired." She rubbed her hand on her lower back for a moment.

"I love that you and Nate are together." I meant it. They were a great couple and had found their way to each other. Finally.

"Sometimes, I still can't believe it."

"When are you due?"

My friend eyed the round curve of her belly. When her eyes lifted to mine, she sighed. "Not until after the holidays."

Our conversation paused when our pizza arrived. I picked up the thread after we had both started eating. "What do you mean you can't believe it? I always thought Nate had a thing for you. I told you that in high school. With Nate being Alex's best friend, you two were thrown together a lot. It was kind of obvious."

"I guess to everybody but me," she said dryly.

"Well, I'm glad you're doing well together."

"Nate's picking me up because I caught a ride here from a friend at work since I didn't drive in this morning. Have you seen him since you've been back?"

I shook my head. "I've been busy cleaning the house and driving to Anchorage to look for new furniture. I cannot deal with the seventies look. I loved Gram, but wow."

Holly let out a peal of laughter just as a rush of cold air came in when someone entered. I reflexively glanced over. The second I saw Rowan, my pulse behaved as if a shot had gone off at the start of a race, bolting out of the gate as fast as it could go. His eyes locked on mine immediately. Sparks ran scattershot through me.

"Well," Holly said before clearing her throat.

I tore my eyes from Rowan's, heat flashing in my cheeks when I looked back at her.

"Well," she repeated.

"Well, what?" I prompted.

"How do you know Rowan?"

I pressed my lips together and let out a sharp sigh. "I knew him in college, if you can believe it. I don't know what the hell he's doing here."

Holly opened her mouth, but I held a hand up. "I know why he's here. That was more of a rhetorical question," I added, irritation pricking at me.

Holly laughed softly. "Okay, so what is the problem with Rowan? Obviously, you have feelings."

Oh, I had feelings, all right. It's just the situation was complicated by an ugly event Rowan didn't even know about.

"We were in college together, and he was one of my closest friends. I kind of had a crush on him, and we went on a few dates. Sort of."

"Sort of? I need more info." Holly took a bite of her pizza, chewing as she waited.

"We had just started dating and then that roommate—remember the one who got on my nerves because every guy was like a challenge to her?"

Holly nodded slowly. "Yeah."

"She flirted with him one night, and I took off." There was so much more to the story, but I wasn't about to go into it here. That might set me off to falling apart, and I couldn't handle that. Not now.

"Did he hook up with her?" my friend pressed, her slice of pizza hovering in the air as she looked over at me.

I shrugged. "I'm not sure."

Holly set her pizza down, her nose scrunching as she eyed me. "Okay, was he a dumbass or not?"

My throat ached, and a familiar panicky feeling tightened in my chest. "Look, that's not all of it. I bolted, and then my night went to hell, and I just couldn't deal with facing Rowan after that. He didn't do anything directly. It's just he's the reminder of something really awful."

Her gaze softened. "Okay. I know a thing or two about trying to forget something awful. Do you want to talk about it?"

Holly had been in a car accident in high school. Her boyfriend had died, and her closest friend had suffered severe burns. That accident had been a marker for all of us back then, and I knew Holly still carried the emotional scars from it.

My gaze dipped down, but I forced my eyes up. "I know you understand, and thank you."

Her nod was nothing more than the barest dip of her chin.

"I definitely don't want to talk about it now." I took a shaky breath, mentally dragging my tattered composure around me.

"Understood."

"It was seven years ago," I added, shaking my head slightly because it annoyed the hell out of me that this was still a *thing* for me.

Holly's eyes searched mine for a moment. "Oh, who's counting?" she commented lightly. "Rowan seems nice. I think you can live with being in town with him." She pressed her lips together, and I knew she was trying not to laugh.

I rolled my eyes. "I can live with Rowan, but I can't freaking believe he's here. What are the chances of that?"

"It's a small world, girl. You know that."

"How do you know Rowan?" I asked, relieved she'd followed my lead to steer this conversation away from deeper, darker waters.

"Because he's friends with Delilah, who's engaged to Alex. He also rents the apartment above their garage," she explained, referring to her twin brother. "He knows Remy Martin too. That's how Delilah ended up here. Remy's sister Shay, who still lives in North Carolina, gave Delilah her tickets for a ski trip because they had to cancel. It was at that ski lodge in Diamond Creek."

"Oh, that's a nice place," I interjected.

"Anyway, Delilah and Alex knew each other from that summer camp he went to in high school in Colorado. Talk about a small world. Anyway, Rowan seems nice. He's got the whole quiet vibe going. I thought he was too serious for my taste, but he's actually kind of funny."

Rowan was quiet and funny, and I missed our friendship so much. I took a bite of pizza, chewing hard as if I could pour my feelings into my food.

When the door to the restaurant opened again, we

both glanced over, and a wide smile broke out across Holly's face.

"Hey, babe!" she called.

"Nate looks just like he did in high school," I said with a grin when she looked back toward me.

"Even a little better, don't you think?"

I chuckled. "Even better."

Nate called over to Holly, "Be there in a minute. I'm picking up takeout since you didn't invite me to dinner." He winked and paused to talk with Rowan.

Just looking at Rowan again sent a prickle of awareness chasing down my spine and heat blooming through me. I shouldn't have been sneaking glances at Rowan, but I was. Nate chatted with him while they waited at the counter. Then they were walking over to our booth together. Fuck my life.

I pasted a bland smile on my face and prayed the tension spinning inside me wasn't obvious.

"How's it going, Mae?" Nate asked when he stopped by our booth before leaning down and dusting a kiss on Holly's cheek.

"Good," I replied politely. "How are you?"

"Right as rain," he offered with a lopsided grin.

When Holly smiled up at him, my heart gave an odd little squeeze. The love in her eyes was so obvious, and I was thrilled for them. I really was. It felt weird to witness such joy because the chances of me having that with anyone were slim to none. I didn't trust myself or the universe.

Even though it would've been easier to pretend Rowan wasn't standing right there, that would only draw attention to me. I turned my tight smile to him, wishing the heat climbing up my neck would dissipate.

He dipped his chin when our eyes met, his lips kicking up into a half grin that sent butterflies spinning in my belly. "How's it going, Mae? All recovered from the fire?"

"I forgot about that," Holly said, slapping her hand on the table. "You were in that fire at the funeral home."

"Yeah, I'm fine. Totally fine," I said quickly before taking a gulp of water. I almost sputtered but managed to swallow without making a mess.

"You saved her, Rowan," Holly said with a dimpled smile.

He chuckled lightly, the sound sending a shiver down my spine. Jesus. *This* man got to me, and it was so freaking annoying.

"It's his job," Nate interjected, his tone dry.

"He still rescued her," Holly added. "You haven't rescued me."

Nate rolled his eyes. "I'm not a firefighter. Would you like me to fly over and drop some water on you?" he teased.

Nate was a pilot. Among other things, he helped out during fire season, flying crews out to the fires and also dropping water and fire retardant in areas where it was needed.

"No, thank you," Holly said pointedly before glancing at Rowan. "I just learned from Mae that you two actually went to college together."

I tore off a bite of pizza, chewing rapidly while I pondered the ways I could get back at her. She studiously didn't look my way. Rowan's gaze bounced from her to me and back again before he nodded. "Yep."

"Small world," Nate commented.

Ugh. I was annoyed with that fucking phrase at this point. "Well, now you can be friends again," Holly offered brightly.

I didn't have a damn thing to say about that. Rowan's eyes met mine, and I could have sworn I saw a flare of heat there. I almost growled at my friend. She was purposely meddling, and I did *not* appreciate it.

Chapter Four

ROWAN

Mae was glaring at Holly, her eyes narrowed and her lips pressed in a tight line. God, she was *so* fucking sexy when she was annoyed. I knew I shouldn't enjoy it. I especially knew I shouldn't be thinking any of these thoughts around her. I still didn't know why, but Mae had cut me out of her life before so completely that I knew something big had happened.

It felt too late to fix it. Yet all I wanted was to make it right, to get back the friend I thought I'd had and find my way back to the only girl I'd ever loved.

Nate chuckled because obviously he knew his wife was up to no good. My name was called from the counter, and I turned away. "Gonna grab my pizza. Good to see you again, Holly," I said with a nod.

Nate's name was called next, and he walked over with me. "What's the scoop on you and Mae?" he asked as soon as we reached the counter again.

"The scoop?"

He grinned. "You can try to play dumb, but clearly, there *is* some history with you two."

I rolled my eyes as I handed cash over to the guy at

the register. "We were in college together. We were good friends and then went on a few dates. After that, she iced me out. I still don't know what I did."

Nate let out a low whistle. "Ouch. Did you try to find out?"

"I tried but never did get the story." My heart felt a burn, and I shifted my shoulders.

"How long ago was that?"

"Seven years."

I hadn't realized Holly had approached. "Wow, you're counting too," she interjected.

I glanced between them, relieved to see that Mae was still at the table. Holly's grin was sly. "Ready to go?" she asked Nate.

"Just waiting to pay. You need me to take care of your check?" he asked.

She shook her head. "I'm going to use the bathroom."

He dipped his head, giving her a lingering kiss before she walked toward the restrooms.

Nate laughed softly. "Watch out for Holly. If she decides she wants to set you two up, she'll make it happen."

"I don't think Mae wants to be set up with me, of all people."

I glanced over my shoulder to see Mae shrugging into her jacket. While Nate was paying, I left my pizza on the counter and went to the restroom. When I returned, Holly and Nate had left, and Mae was nowhere to be found.

"Dammit," I muttered to myself, grabbing the pizza box and hurrying out to the parking lot. She was stopped beside a car, fishing her keys out of her purse. She was conveniently parked right beside mine.

"Mae!" I called.

She turned. "What?" she muttered as I stopped between our vehicles.

I opened my passenger door quickly and slid the pizza in.

"Look, this is a small town, and I'd like to be friends," I said quickly.

"We're friends. It's fine." Her tone was careful, and her eyes landed somewhere around my cheek.

"Is it fine?"

She blinked up at me, and it felt as if a charge lit the air between us.

"Sure." She shrugged. "I think it's fine. It's been years. It was college. Whatever."

I rested my hand on the top of her car. "Mae, I honestly don't know what happened." Frustration churned inside me because I felt as if I were shadow-boxing here, and I had no idea what I was facing.

It was just dark enough in the parking lot that I couldn't tell, but I could've sworn Mae's eyes glittered with tears. Her lashes swept down, and she took a shaky breath. When she looked back at me, her expression was careful. "At that party, I saw you with Sharon."

I stared at her blankly, picking through my recollections. It took a minute, but I recalled Sharon flirting aggressively that night and even trying to kiss me. "When she made a move on me? Mae, nothing happened. *Nothing*."

Mae's mouth twisted in a weary smile, and bitterness chased in her eyes. "She made a move on any guy she thought I liked. That was her thing. We were only roommates for a semester. I didn't like that many guys, anyway."

This still didn't make sense. "Mae, you vented to me about her. You have to know I'd never do that."

We stared at each other, and Mae shivered slightly. I didn't know what Mae wasn't telling me, but this wasn't why she stopped talking to me. She lifted her keys and tapped the fob. Her engine started up. "I want the car to be warm when I get in," she explained.

I hadn't realized I'd instinctively stepped closer to her. "I don't think you're telling me everything, but maybe you will someday." A part of me was frustrated, almost angry, but I knew her well enough that I knew she was uncomfortable with something. Pressure wouldn't solve it. Not now, not here, in a parking lot in the winter.

She took another breath before dipping her chin, just barely, to acknowledge my comment.

"How have you been? I'm sorry about your grandmother."

"Thank you," she said quietly.

We were standing there, staring at each other, while her car engine hummed. I thought I wanted to kiss her. Actually, I didn't think I wanted to kiss her. I really fucking wanted to kiss her. The need was fierce.

She opened her mouth to say something, and reason and thought fled me in the chilly darkness. I closed the distance between us in a flash. She *was* cold after all, but her lips were warm. She let out a surprised sound when I brushed mine over hers.

I thought this would be when she shoved me away, but she didn't. Her mouth opened underneath mine, and I couldn't resist sliding my hand in her silky, honeyed locks. I angled my head to the side and slipped my tongue into the warm sweetness of her mouth. It had been a full seven years since I kissed Mae, but it felt like just yesterday as the sensations from back then came rushing back.

Sweet hell. Her lips were soft and plump, and her

tongue glided against mine in a searching tease. It felt as if lightning sizzled through my entire system.

Headlights arced across us, and she jumped back, breaking the kiss abruptly. "Oh!" Her hand flew to her chest.

Even though there wasn't much light out here in the parking lot, I knew her cheeks were pink, and I wanted to kiss her again. Her shoulders rose and fell with her rapid breathing, and it felt as if the air around us was crackling with electricity.

"Mae," I began just as another car turned into the parking lot.

"I have to go," she said. Moving swiftly, she opened her car door and slipped in.

She lifted her hand in a quick wave while I tried to absorb the sensations rioting through me. I watched as she drove away, her taillights glowing red down the road after she turned out of the parking lot. An icy gust of wind blew, nudging me out of my stunned haze. I climbed into my SUV and blasted the heat because it was freezing.

I drove home, my thoughts turning over what Mae had shared about her college roommate, the one who'd made such a bold pass at me. Since I'd ignored her, I hadn't thought much of it beyond that I meant to tell Mae it happened. Honestly, if she hadn't been Mae's roommate, if I hadn't been best friends with Mae and secretly in love with her, I wouldn't have even remembered that pass or that girl. It had been at a crowded party, the cacophony of people around me hazing out everything else.

I still knew Mae wasn't telling me everything. I sensed it in my gut, down to my bones. It hurt that she wouldn't just tell me. Fuck.

Chapter Five

MAE

"So, this data is yours," Scott said, gesturing his hand in a small arc.

We were seated at a U-shaped desk, which had an array of computer monitors lining the surface and encircling us. I felt my lips curling into a smile.

"This is awesome." I let out a happy sigh.

Scott chuckled as I glanced toward him. "Isn't it, though?"

Scott Rogers was another professor here at the university. While he wasn't my boss, he'd been assigned to show me around. I worked in environmental and marine sciences with a focus on oceans.

I loved it. Having grown up in Alaska with fishing as part of my childhood, I cared deeply about making sure we had sustainable fisheries. Water comprised approximately seventy percent of the Earth's surface, and the oceans held more than ninety-six percent of that water. It was critical for them to stay healthy.

Alaska was one of the last frontiers as far as fisheries went in North America. It was one of the few places with well-protected fisheries, yet it was a constant battle here.

My grandfather had lived his life fishing. Summer days spent on the rivers and going out fishing in the ocean were some of my favorite childhood memories. Yet climate change was real. It was coming fast and furious here in Alaska. Glaciers that were once visible from the highway in Alaska had receded out of view with so many more changes galloping toward us.

"Basically, just take your time going through this data. Each data set contains different rivers, bays, and fish runs coming in from the ocean and so on," Scott was explaining, referencing fish tracking. "We also have cross-comparisons to data shared from other countries and all over the US. And old data from different fisheries. It's a lot."

He chuckled again when I began clicking through the screens to look around, bouncing from one computer screen to the next. "Slow your roll. You've got plenty of time. So what brought you here?" he asked next.

I thought I detected a hint of interest from Scott, but I wasn't sure. He was handsome with clean-cut features and an outdoorsy vibe. He had rich brown hair and eyes to match. I tried to mentally assess if there was any attraction for me, but there was nothing, not even a little zing of curiosity. I'd done that for years because I found it nearly impossible to experience chemistry. One tragic night robbed me of that, blockading my instincts behind a wall of fear and distrust.

I couldn't help it, but my mind conjured up Rowan with his almost black hair and piercing green eyes. Merely imagining him elicited a flash of fiery heat while I couldn't evoke anything even resembling heat to anyone else. I didn't want to get involved with anybody I worked with, but it would have been nice to feel some sort of attraction. My internal sigh was weary and resigned.

Why, oh why, did Rowan have to light my fire so fiercely?

"Mae?" Scott prompted, fortunately oblivious to my mental ramblings.

What had he asked me? Oh, right, why here. "I grew up in Willow Brook and wanted to come back to Alaska."

"Ah, Alaska born and bred then," he said with a quick nod.

"Absolutely. I love fishing, and I love the ocean. That's what led me into environmental and marine sciences. I'm thrilled to be back here and to actually be doing this job, right here at the cutting edge, so to speak. I don't know if that's good or bad. With the shifts in the weather, things are already changing fast here, and I'm very concerned about the effects of warmer ocean temperatures on salmon spawning."

"You and everyone who tracks what happens in the ocean," he commented dryly. His phone vibrated, and he patted his shirt pocket, slipping it out and glancing down. "I need to take this." He stood from the desk, rapping his knuckles lightly on the surface. "You know where to reach me if you have any questions about syllabi, classes, and so on."

"I do. Thank you for showing me around today."

"If I don't see you in the hallways before then, I'll see you at the staff meeting on Friday."

I smiled and waved as he left the room. I lost myself in data for a few hours as I familiarized myself with the various computer systems at my fingertips here. Thank God I'd set an alarm on my phone for my first class because I would have lost track of time.

———

"How was your first week?" my mother asked, smiling at me from across the table.

"It was good. Actually, it was really good. I'm glad I decided to take the job." I lifted my glass of water and took a swallow.

My mother had wanted to get pizza, so she'd asked me to go with her to Alpenglow Pizza. I only hoped Rowan didn't happen to stop by while we were here. It had been a few days since our kiss, and I'd replayed it too many times in my mind. I'd also seen him in town almost every single day, which was frustrating. Even though I was working in Anchorage, I liked to grab coffee at Firehouse Café. I also had to go to the grocery store, and apparently, so did he. I also knew he went to the same gas station I did, and he was staying in the apartment above the garage at Delilah and Alex's place, which was a mere three houses down from my grandmother's house. Willow Brook was truly a small town, and I would have to get used to seeing Rowan.

I kept telling myself the embers that had started to flicker into flames from that kiss would cool soon. That didn't seem to be happening. Seeing Rowan everywhere wasn't helping matters at all. I forced my attention back to my mother.

"I'm glad you're here," she said, reaching over and squeezing my hand on the table.

With the exception of Rowan's presence, I was glad to be home. I'd missed it. I was an Alaskan girl through and through, and no other place felt like home.

My mom's honey-blond hair, which I had inherited, had faded and had silver streaks mingling through the blond. Her eyes were a darker shade of brown than mine.

We chatted a bit about the town and her life before our pizza arrived. The server set it on the raised stand in the center of the table, checking to see if we needed anything else before he left. I had just lifted a slice of pizza when my mother commented, "So, I heard an old friend of yours from college moved here."

I lowered the pizza. "Huh?"

My mother's eyes twinkled as she lifted one shoulder in a delicate shrug. "I heard it from Maisie when I saw her at the store. He's on the new firefighter crew."

I took a bite of pizza, nodding and making some sort of humming sound. My mother, because she was gracious enough not to push the matter, started eating. After a few minutes, she added, "I worry about you, hon. You never date."

I eyed her suspiciously and almost reached for another piece of pizza, but I was full. With a sigh, I replied, "I'm not really focused on dating."

I'd never told my parents what happened in college. A few college friends knew and the therapist I'd seen. I really didn't want to be slinging the events of that night around. As much as I tried not to have it define me, I also knew that by choosing silence, I had, in some ways, given it more power.

The desperate wish for someone to be there for me had morphed into me not wanting to rely on anyone.

Ever. My thoughts circled back to Rowan, and I braced myself against them.

Aside from all he didn't know, he'd been one of the best friends I'd ever had, and I'd really started to fall for him. That spark had burned hot and still did.

My mother's voice brought me back to the moment. "I know you haven't been focused on that, and I'm not one to pry or push, but I worry because I feel like something happened."

I shrugged lightly because no way in hell would I talk about it here, if ever. "I'm fine, Mom."

She studied me quietly before dabbing at her mouth with a napkin. "Well, I hope you'll find someone if you want that."

"Mom, if I meet someone and it feels right, then yes, I want that. Until then, don't worry about it. I'm focused on being back home, back where I want to be. I have a job that I love. That's a lot more than some people have. I like being single," I insisted, which was true but also not really true. Being single was safe. What I craved was feeling safe with someone else, and I didn't believe that was possible.

As I lay in bed later that night, I replayed that stupid kiss with Rowan yet again. Why did I tell him about seeing my roommate hit on him? Now, I felt even more ridiculous because there was one detail Rowan didn't know, and only one other person knew. Back in college, I'd still been a virgin, and the only person who'd known that back then was that roommate, the one who'd hit on him. Because like an idiot, before I realized just how she was, we'd been friendly. I wanted to bond with my college roommate. One night after a few too many margaritas at a bar, I'd fessed up that I'd never gone there with any guy.

She took advantage of that because she was always

willing to go there. I wasn't shaming her. I just hated how she used it to hurt me. Rowan was the third guy I had started to date that she made a move on. I wondered if he'd been telling me the truth the other night, that it had never gone further than what I saw. I would always have to wonder.

"Get out of my head, Rowan," I said to the ceiling.

The ceiling had nothing to say in return.

Chapter Six

ROWAN

"Colbie, are you okay?" I asked.

Colbie let out a very deep sigh, but then my sixteen-year-old sister was the master of sighs, usually dramatic and overblown. "Yes, I'm okay. Why are you asking?"

"Why do you think I'm asking?" I returned, tapping the credit card screen at the gas station as I held the phone in one hand and waited for the receipt to print for the gas I'd just gotten.

Another sigh filtered through the phone line. "Because Mom and Dad don't like my new boyfriend."

She was spot-on. Our mother had, in fact, shared her worries about my sister's new boyfriend with me just the other day. That wasn't the only reason I was calling my sister, but part of it. I wasn't going to tell her she was right, though. "Why don't they like your new boyfriend?" Even though I knew what my parents thought, I wanted to hear my sister's perception of the situation.

"Dad thinks he's controlling, and Mom had a talk with me the other night."

I chuckled because I, too, had been subjected to my mother's talks when I was a teenager. I didn't miss those even though I adored my mother. "What was this talk about? Fill me in."

Even though I was also worried about my sister's new boyfriend because my parents weren't stupid, I was going to stay connected to her because it wouldn't help a thing to alienate her from all of us.

"She talked to me about birth control and scheduled an appointment with my doctor. She wants to make sure I'm on the pill or something." The affront in Colbie's tone rang through the line.

I had to grit my teeth at that. Obviously, with my sister being sixteen years old, it was possible she was sexually active, but I fucking did *not* want to think about that. Nor did I want to think about any guy who wanted to have sex with her because I might have to punch him right in the face. I suppose it was good I was in Alaska and over four thousand miles away from Stolen Hearts Valley. I took a breath, marshaling my composure as I tucked the receipt in my pocket and climbed in my SUV.

"Okay, she had the birth control talk. I'm familiar with that," I said, keeping my tone level and casual even though I didn't feel that way at all inside. "What else?"

"Oh, Lord, she talked to me about consent and my body and loving myself and gave me this whole talk about red flags in relationships. Larry is not an asshole. He just really likes me. I'm special. That's what he told me. He's the first guy who ever told me that."

Alarms were blaring in my brain. "Tell me what he said. Exactly. And, of course, you're special."

"Yeah, I'm your little sister. Jesus. Plus, I was an

accident way after Mom thought she couldn't have kids anymore, so you're too old to be annoyed with me."

I laughed softly. "True story. Anyway, back to Larry. What did he say?"

"He said he can't help himself. I'm really special to him, so he has to make sure I'm okay. That's why Dad thinks he's controlling. He likes me to share my location with him, so we're on that app."

Anger rolled through me. My spidey sense was tingling, big time. "Oh, yeah? What app?"

"You know, the one we share. I tracked your drive all the way to Alaska."

Oh, thank fuck. It was the same app, and we were already connected.

"All right, what else?"

"He worries about my friends because he doesn't want anyone to take advantage of me."

"Like your girlfriends?"

"No, my guy friends," Colbie explained.

"Even Trent?" I prompted. Trent was one of Colbie's best friends and had been since they were little. They were practically brother and sister, and I'd seen them together many times. There was no *there* there. They were truly just friends.

"Jealousy can be weird, so be careful about that," I added, trying to keep my tone casual. Jesus, who the fuck was Larry, and what was I going to do about him? He was new to town. Even my mother admitted he was handsome.

Colbie sighed. Again. "I know. It's not jealousy. He's just protective."

"What does Trent think of him?" I asked. I hoped that might elicit some sort of reaction from my sister.

"I don't know," she said, her tone careful.

"You still hanging out with Trent?"

"Uh, some."

Ah, fuck. I was not feeling good about this, but there was nothing for me to do, even if I was there. It wasn't like I could barge in and tell my sister who she could and couldn't date.

"You just remember someone who really cares about you also cares about the people who matter to you," I finally said, thinking that was pretty lame, but it was all I could think of.

My sister called me out. "Nice try, Rowan. Obviously, I know that. Anyway, what's up with you? How's Alaska?"

"It's good. I like it so far."

"Are you coming home for Thanksgiving?" she asked as I drove toward home. Thanksgiving was weeks away.

"I'm not sure. It's either Thanksgiving or Christmas. I need to talk to my boss about which holiday I can take off, but I'll talk to Mom and Dad first. How's that sound?"

"Good. I miss you," she said.

"I miss you too. So, tell me. How's Mom?"

My sister went quiet for a moment, her voice soft when she replied, "I think she's okay. You know, they don't talk to me about her medical stuff. I just know when she's had chemo because she's exhausted afterward."

My stomach twisted, and worry churned. "All right. Stay in touch now. Okay?"

"Always," she retorted.

"Mom around?"

"Yeah, she's cooking dinner. You called me on my cell," she pointed out.

"I don't suppose you'd hand it over to her," I countered dryly.

"No, I have other things to do with my phone, and I'm all the way upstairs. Call the house phone."

I chuckled. "Love ya, sis. Talk soon."

I waited to call my parents' house number until I pulled into my driveway. Even though both of my parents used cell phones, they still relied on the house phone for regular calls. I could picture it mounted on the kitchen wall in my mind's eye. It rang twice before my mother answered while I walked up the stairs to my apartment.

"Hey, Rowan."

"Hey, Mom. How's it going?"

"Good, good. You?"

"I'm fine. I talked to Colbie. I don't have a good feeling about this guy." I tucked the phone against one shoulder as I walked into my apartment and closed the door behind me, immediately crossing the room to check the thermostat.

My mother clucked. "That's why your father mentioned him to you. I don't know what to do. I know if we forbid her from seeing him, it's not going to go well."

"Of course not. Just keep an eye on her."

"Please keep calling her."

"Of course, Mom. I call her anyway."

"I know. She listens to you in a way she doesn't with your father and me."

"I get it." I paused and took a breath. "So, what's up with the big C?"

"I'm fine," my mother replied, almost too quickly. She preferred to gloss over her medical concerns. She hated anyone worrying about her.

"Are you really?" I pressed.

My mother had been diagnosed with breast cancer. She had an initial round of treatment years ago, and they'd declared her cancer-free only to have it return six years later.

"I *am* fine."

"Would you tell me if you weren't, Mom?"

"I would. You know I would," she insisted.

"If you need me to come home—" I began.

"No," my mother said sharply. "We are thrilled you're out in Alaska. Keep sending pictures, and we're going to come visit when I get through this."

"All right, Mom. Just know I'll come home in a second if you need me."

"I know you will. I love you," she said firmly.

"Love you too. Also, I'm going to talk to my boss and figure out if I'll be there for Thanksgiving or Christmas."

"Either one works for us. We just want to see your face and give you a big hug."

We said our goodbyes, and I tapped to end the call. After setting my phone on the coffee table, I crossed my small apartment and leaned my hands on the windowsill to look out.

Delilah Taylor hailed from my hometown, Stolen Hearts Valley, North Carolina, just as Remy did. Delilah and her fiancé had offered me the garage apartment until I found a better place. It was a nice place with a large open living room, an efficiency kitchen, a full bath, and an actual bedroom. Like most of Alaska, it also had a sweet view of the mountains.

Snow had begun to fall this afternoon and was picking up its pace. We were working on over a foot. Alex had already plowed the driveway once by the time I got home.

My mind spun to Mae. She was always waiting

along the edges of my thoughts. I couldn't seem to go more than a day without seeing her somewhere in town, and she always looked flustered and cute. I wanted the chance to have more of a conversation with her. Hell, I wanted a chance with her. She had an edge to her that hadn't been there before. She felt like a wild animal about to bolt whenever I encountered her.

Glancing at my watch, I strode to the kitchen to check my food options. Our crew had four days off, so I might as well stock up. I snagged my wallet and my down jacket and headed out again. I should've thought to check this morning, but it wasn't too late yet. I had only discovered a few days ago that Mae lived just down the street from me. When I commented on it to Alex, he'd mentioned she'd inherited her grandmother's house. I had wanted to ask Alex so many more questions about Mae, but I didn't feel right about it. He knew her since childhood whereas I'd known her for only a few years. We'd been close our first three years of college together, and that was it. That span of time loomed large in my memory and packed a punch.

After I began driving, I slowed when I saw a figure shoveling Mae's driveway. I slowed and pulled over. "Mae!" I called through the snow.

She turned, trudging through the snow to stop beside my open window. "Yeah?"

"You're gonna shovel that whole driveway?"

My eyes bounced to her car where it sat parked at the end, roughly a quarter mile from the road. She shrugged. "Yeah."

"You're joking, right?"

"No," she countered, her tone prickly.

"I'm plowing your driveway, Mae." I looked toward the end of the driveway to see an old truck with a big plow mounted on the front. "Is your plow truck broken?"

She let out a put-upon sigh. "It won't start."

"Get in," I said. "Just put your shovel on the back seat."

I was surprised when she didn't argue and climbed in. When I turned into her driveway, she asked, "Are you just driving through this?"

"It's not that bad. I have plenty of clearance with four-wheel drive. Why don't you just call someone to plow? Or I can borrow Alex's plow if you need help."

"I can shovel," she muttered.

I decided against pointing out how quickly she'd hopped in my SUV. "Do you mind if I try to start your truck? Is that your truck anyway?"

"Well, it's my grandmother's old truck. I haven't switched over the registration, but all I'm planning to do with it is plow."

"You probably don't need to change the registration if you're not driving it off your property. Let me see if I can start it for you. Have you ever plowed a driveway?"

Mae's silence gave me the answer. "I'll take that as a no. Will you let me plow it for you if I can start the truck? If not, I can borrow Alex's."

She crossed her arms. "Fine." I tried not to chuckle, but I couldn't help it. "What's so funny?"

"Nothing, really."

"Well then, why did you laugh?" she pressed.

"Because you're kind of stubborn sometimes," I replied honestly.

Her response was something between a snort and a growl. I came to a stop at the end of the driveway. The plow truck was parked in a small parking area off to the side.

"You can wait here, or go in the house while I check it out."

"Well, I need to get my car."

I glanced at her car where the snow was piled up behind it. "Give me your keys, and I'll get your car."

Mae started to protest, "Rowan, I can—"

I cut in, "Do you really want to sit here and argue with me about this? I can take care of it, probably in a few minutes, if I can start the truck."

"All right, all right," she muttered.

Chapter Seven

ROWAN

Mae handed me her keys, and I waited while she went inside. I was pretty handy with mechanics. While my dad wasn't a mechanic by trade, he took care of most of his own car maintenance and enjoyed refurbishing old vehicles. I'd learned all the basics from him. It only took a minute to deduce all this ancient truck needed was a jumpstart. After getting it running, I plowed the drive inside of a few minutes and moved my vehicle to park beside the plow truck before I made sure to clear the area right behind Mae's car.

When I walked to her door, it swung open just as I lifted my hand to knock. I didn't realize I was cold until she commented, "Get in here. You're shivering."

I wasn't going to argue because I would take any chance to spend time with Mae. I looked around once I got inside. "Nice place," I said when my eyes made their way back to hers.

Mae's lips twitched at the corners. "It's okay, you can say it."

"Say what?"

"It's like entering a time warp. There's still shag

carpet on the floor and look at that furniture." She swung her arm in an arc.

There was, in fact, bright green shag carpet in the living room, and the furniture did look straight out of the seventies, all bright colors and boxy shapes. I shrugged when my eyes met hers again. "Hey, it's got character."

"I made some hot chocolate for you."

"You did?" This surprised me.

"Yes. We're friends, right?"

I looked into her ginger eyes, and it felt as if sparks began to shimmer in the air around us, heating the space. "Yeah, you said we were fine. Fine is never good."

Mae looked away. Her gaze dipped to the ground and then back up. "Here." She pointed at a coat rack by the door. "You can hang your coat up and take your boots off. I'll give you some hot chocolate, but I'm not gonna let you tromp snow all over the place."

I followed her instructions, toeing my boots off by the door and hanging my jacket up, smiling at the bright painted wooden daisy atop the coat rack. I followed her through an archway to the side of the living room that led into a dining area and another archway that led into the kitchen. Despite the dated furnishings, the house was cute. My mom would have said it had good bones—everything was well maintained and tidy.

Mae gestured to a round table by the windows, and I took a seat. She filled two mugs and walked over. After she set the mugs down, she moved to sit down across from me before she jumped up. "Do you want something in that?"

"What's something?" I prompted.

She pressed her lips together. "I don't know, a dash of chocolate vodka or some mint liqueur."

"Well, I'll never say no to that. Both sound good," I returned.

She fetched a bottle out of the cabinet, pouring a generous dollop in both mugs before sitting down. I didn't know what she'd been wearing before, but now she looked absolutely adorable. She was wearing a fluffy pink sweater with fitted leggings and pink socks to match. Her hair was pulled up in a bun with loose tendrils framing her face. As I looked over at her, my eyes lingered on her pink cheeks. There was something almost innocent about her, but not really. Somehow, she was wholesome and sensual at the same time.

"Thank you for fixing the truck and plowing my driveway," she said after she took a swallow of her hot chocolate.

"Happy to help. It was just a dead battery."

"Now, you can plow me out anytime," she said, her lips twitching at the corners.

"Just ask, and I'll be here," I said, meaning that on more levels than I guessed she'd suspect.

I paused to take a swallow of the hot chocolate. "Oh, this is good," I said as I lowered the mug. There was the smooth burn of minty liqueur mingling with the rich chocolate. "Not too sweet."

"I don't like mine too sweet."

"You make your own?"

Mae nodded. "I do." When my brows hitched in surprise, she added, "All you need is actual cocoa and some sugar and milk."

"It's definitely better than the kind in the little packets that I use." I took another swallow. "How are you?" I asked a moment later.

Mae lifted her shoulder in an elegant shrug. "I'm fine."

Ah, there we were with fine. I decided to press ahead. "So, you came home because your grandmother passed away?"

Her shoulders rose when she took a breath and let it out quickly. "Yes."

"I'm sorry about that."

"Again, thank you. She lived a good life. I miss her, but it wasn't unexpected. She'd been sick."

"How old was she?"

Mae drummed her fingertips on the table and took another swallow of hot chocolate. "Eighty-two, I think."

"Well, that's a good long life."

Her smile was quick, and my heart warmed. "It definitely was. So, how did you end up here?"

"Didn't I tell you Remy told me about the job?"

"Oh, that's right! You did. The world is weirdly small, isn't it?" Her tone was bright with a touch of force to it.

"I never thought I'd see you again," I said, deciding to be direct.

"No, I don't suppose you did."

"If I need to apologize for Sharon hitting on me, I'll do it as much as I need to."

Her cheeks went a little pink, and she shook her head. "It's okay, it was seven years ago. You weren't the only guy she made a move on. She was kind of busy."

"Busy? Is that what you call it?"

"I don't know what to call it. We didn't stay friends. I don't know if we really were friends to begin with."

I nodded because there wasn't much else to offer on that.

"Anyway, here you are, on my turf now." She lifted her chin slightly, a saucy look in her eyes.

"I guess I am."

"Are you staying in Willow Brook?"

I really wanted to know the answer to that question, and I didn't want to think too much about why. The very girl who'd consumed my thoughts off and on over the years was sitting right here in front of me.

"For now," I said honestly because now was all we had. "Tell me about your life, Mae."

"Tell me what you remember." Her eyes narrowed.

I didn't mind meeting the challenge because I remembered a lot about Mae. She was smart and really into biology and the environment. "Let me guess. You went into some kind of science career."

Her mouth dropped open before she snapped it shut, pressing her lips together tightly. "How do you know that?" she finally asked.

"Because we met in that environmental sciences class. You loved it. I mean, you *really* loved it."

She rolled her eyes. "I did. Is that so bad?"

"Not at all. I thought it was great. It's good to be passionate about something. So, tell me what you do now?"

"Well, I did go into environmental science with a focus on oceans. I grew up around fishing, and Alaska is, at least in North America, ground zero for climate change. I took a position at a university in Anchorage."

"That sounds perfect for you. It doesn't surprise me."

"You ended up becoming a hotshot firefighter."

"Does that surprise you?"

Her cheeks went pink as she shook her head. "No,

you were into outdoorsy stuff. That's a great career for that. You get to be outdoors a lot."

I nodded. "Winter's a quiet time. That's good, though. We work our asses off during fire season, so having some downtime is pretty important."

We chatted a bit more about mundane life stuff, and it was really nice to spend time with Mae. Not that I'd forgotten, but it was a reminder of why I liked her before. She had a subtle, sly sense of humor under-laid with a sweetness. I recalled how nervous I'd been to ask her out after we'd been friends and the sheer relief that she'd wanted the same thing. We'd never gotten past a few kisses, though.

Somewhere in that conversation, I discovered she was hoarding the last season of *Schitt's Creek*. "You haven't seen it?" I asked, incredulous.

"No, because then I'll watch it, and it'll be over," she insisted.

"Then you can watch the whole show again. Come on, we should start it."

"We should?" She eyed me dubiously, and I wanted to kiss her.

"Yes," I insisted. "Do you have Netflix?"

"Of course, I do."

"Come on, Mae. I love that show. I want to see it with you."

"All right, let me make some more hot chocolate."

And, that was how I found myself sitting on her couch with the original reason for leaving my apart-ment completely forgotten because hanging out with Mae in the time warp of her grandmother's house was exactly where I wanted to be.

Three episodes later, Mae's feet were curled up under her knees and her scent was drifting to me. She smelled sweet, kind of like vanilla. And, fuck me, I wanted to kiss her all over again.

Glancing over at her, I asked, "What would it take to get you to go to dinner with me?"

"We just had hot chocolate and watched three episodes of *Schitt's Creek*. I think that's more than dinner," she said, a subtle laugh lacing her words.

Angling to face her, I nodded. "We did, but I still want to take you to dinner."

"You know how small this town is, right?" she prompted.

"Yeah," I said slowly. "Is that a problem?"

"I don't know. Gossip is probably harder to put out here than those fires you fight in the summer," she said bluntly.

I threw my head back with a laugh. Our empty mugs sat on the coffee table. Her stomach growled, and she slapped her hand over it. I grinned. "Maybe we should order pizza."

"Then we have to go get it," she pointed out.

"No, we can get it delivered."

"We can?" She seemed shocked at this.

"Yeah, of course we can."

"Oh, my god," she breathed. "Willow Brook never had delivery when I was growing up here."

"Well, the pizza place delivers. I can guarantee it. They've come to my place, which is just down the street."

Chapter Eight

ROWAN

We ordered pizza, and the only downside was it was going to be a whole hour before it'd be here because there was a snowstorm and they were backed up. A big snowstorm was money time for the pizza delivery business.

After I ordered, I was in the kitchen where Mae had sent me to get a glass of water when she went to the bathroom. I had just set my phone on the counter when she stopped in the archway.

"Well?"

"Well, what?"

She narrowed her eyes and pursed her lips. She was too fucking cute. I'd fallen for Mae in college for lots of reasons, and everything about her now felt as if it was in sharper focus.

"Did you order the pizza, or were they closed?"

"Of course, they're not closed. As far as I can tell, nothing closes here when it snows. You should know. You're the one who grew up in Alaska."

Mae let out a throaty laugh, and lust sizzled like lightning through my body. She took a few more steps into the kitchen, resting her hips against the counter and curling her hands on the edge beside her hips. "That's true. Nothing does close around here, but I've been away long enough I forgot. What are winters like in the mountains in North Carolina?"

"We get snow and ice. But it doesn't get as cold as here. You lived through some winters in North Carolina."

"Not in the mountains," Mae countered. "Chapel Hill isn't exactly cold."

I grinned as I crossed over to her. "No, it's not." Stopping in front of her, I lifted a hand and caught a lock of hair dangling on her cheek. I let it slide, soft and silky, through my fingers.

The little hitch in her breath sent another sizzle through my body. I decided this time I would ask because I needed to know. I wasn't just being impulsive.

"I'd like to kiss you." Her breath caught in her throat again before she swallowed. "What do you think about that?"

Mae's ginger eyes blinked. "About you kissing me?" she returned in a husky whisper.

"Yes."

When she took a breath this time, her breasts brushed against my chest. "Okay."

I started to lean forward, and then she placed her palm over my chest. My heart lunged, thudding against the heat of her touch.

Chapter Nine

MAE

"Why do you want to kiss me?" I heard myself asking.

My mind silently volleyed a question back at me. *Really? You're going to ruin Rowan wanting to kiss you?*

Well, yeah, I was. What we'd had before loomed large in my memory—the intensity of my crush on him when we were friends, and my worries he didn't return the feeling followed by sheer joy upon learning he did. A few hot kisses and then feeling as if life had thrown a boulder at me. Emotionally, that is. I'd been crushed and ashamed and hadn't known how to climb out from under the weight of what happened that fated night. No matter how many times I tried to remind myself Rowan had nothing to do with it, he was entwined in the dark memory because he was the reason I'd been there that night.

I opened my mouth to clarify, but he beat me to it.

"Because I want to kiss you. So, so much. You're the only person I've wanted to kiss in a long time, and I want this chance with you."

"What does that mean?" I pressed. I hated the

vulnerability rising swiftly inside me. I hoped it didn't show in my voice and on my face.

"Just that you're the only girl I want to kiss, and I'm not about to let you slip away again. I won't rush, but I don't think I'm alone in how I feel. Am I? Just tell me if I am."

I stared into his green eyes, my heart hammering in my chest and desire rushing through me. "You're not," I whispered, the words slipping out before my defenses could stop them.

"Okay?"

I swallowed and nodded. The next few seconds felt interminable because my impatience had me nearly vibrating. Whether he sensed my restless need or not, he took his sweet time. He caught that loose lock of hair again, spinning it around his fingers and tucking it behind my ear. His calloused fingertips brushed along my sensitive skin, and goose bumps rose in a prickling rush with a hot shiver chasing down my spine.

His hand slid over the curve of my shoulder and then down around my waist as he stepped closer. His palm came flat against my back, just above the dip of my waist. He took another step, and then I could feel the heat of him from head to toe. He palmed my cheek with his free hand, his thumb sliding across my bottom lip. I almost let out a sob of impatience when his intense green eyes bored into mine. It felt as if he was peeling back all of my layers and exposing me. And we hadn't even kissed yet.

My belly swooped when he finally dipped his head, and his lips brushed across mine. It felt as if a flame leaped from him to me, binding us together in the scorch of heat.

He didn't hurry. Not at all. After another brush of

his lips, he angled my head to the side before he fit his mouth over mine. His tongue finally, *finally* glided in as I let out a little moan. What started out slow got hot and wild really fast. We burst into flames together, our tongues tangling, our breath mingling, and the heat of him hard against me.

I had no idea how long I clung to him, one arm sliding around his muscled shoulders as my other palm explored the hard planes of his chest. Somewhere along the way, one of us needed air, so we broke free. The sound of our ragged breathing was loud in the quiet kitchen.

Rowan's eyes met mine, and he looked as stunned as I felt. "Mae," he rasped, his tone almost wondering.

"What?" I whispered.

He shook his head slightly, and I felt the brush of his thumb on the side of my neck, just over the rapid flutter of my pulse. My body felt prickly all over as if I couldn't contain the sensations ricocheting through me. I was slick with need and shifted my thighs, rubbing them together, unconsciously attempting to relieve the ache there. His eyes darkened as he stared at me. Then his mouth was on mine again. We tumbled into kiss after kiss after kiss as we explored each other.

My hand found its way under the hem of his shirt. His skin was hot to the touch, and I sighed when his hand finally brushed over the curve of my belly. I could feel the calloused surface of his palm, a contrast to my skin. He was all hard with rough edges while I felt soft. I was wearing my most comfortable clothes, and I wanted all of them to be thrown free. I cried out at the feel of him cupping my bare breast. My nipples were so tight they hurt when he teased his thumb across one. I could feel his arousal like a brand through his jeans.

He muttered something, and then he was shoving my sweater off. I didn't even know where it fell. All I knew was I needed more. I needed him. I needed everything.

I cried out sharply at the feel of his mouth closing over a nipple. He gave it just enough suction that the sharp pleasure arrowed straight to the core of me, and my pussy clenched. I needed relief badly. I heard him saying something indecipherable, followed by, "Let me take care of you."

I was frantic for him to take care of me. I couldn't say that because I couldn't form a single word, but I was relieved when he lifted me onto the counter. I felt his hand sliding past the waistband of my cotton pants and delving between my thighs. I was wet, so, *so* wet. I couldn't think. I was *made* of need.

His fingers slipped through my folds, and I was already rocking into him, desperate for something, anything to relieve the pressure. I felt him lift his head. "Mae?"

I rocked into his touch, whimpering.

"Mae?" he repeated.

I finally dragged my eyes open. "Fuck, you're gorgeous," he murmured, just as he sank two fingers in me. I couldn't look away from the beam of his gaze, the sound of my heartbeat rushing through me.

I moaned as my channel clenched around him. "Come for me," he said bluntly. I couldn't do anything except stare as he drew his fingers out and thrust them in again. His thumb swirled around my swollen, slippery wet clit. I clung to him as he fucked me with his fingers. My mind blanked, and I cried out when pleasure ricocheted sharply through me.

My eyes closed, and my forehead fell to the curve of his neck. I breathed him in as sensations rolled through me. He had a crisp musky scent, and I thought I might never forget it.

Chapter Ten

ROWAN

Mae had residual tremors running through her, and I could feel the soft gust of her breath against my neck. I breathed her in, absorbing the feel of her all soft in my arms. I was startled at how fast this had spiraled. I just meant to kiss her, but I'd felt her need digging into me like claws, and I wanted to give her that release. I was almost in awe at how raw and unguarded she'd been with me.

After a moment, I felt her lift her head. Although my lids were heavy, I dragged my eyes open. She blinked, her gaze as stunned as mine probably was.

"Oh," she said.

"That's one way to put it." Reluctantly, I drew my fingers out of the very heart of her and pulled her cotton underwear back in place. With my other hand, I brushed her mussed hair away from her forehead.

"I didn't mean..." I stopped when she shook her head.

"I don't know what you didn't mean, but I wanted that." A wash of pink crested high on her cheeks, and my heart contracted in a sweet, aching twist.

We stared at each other in that quiet moment, and something bloomed in the air between us. I didn't know what it was. It felt ephemeral, intense, almost as if I couldn't grab onto it, yet its power shimmered around us.

The doorbell rang, the sound abrupt and snapping through the moment. Mae's eyes flew wide, her palm flying to her chest.

"They can't see us, Mae. The door's closed, and we're in the kitchen." My lips tugged into a smile.

She pressed her lips together and rolled her eyes. "I know, I know. It just startled me. Can you hand me my sweater?"

I reluctantly stepped away from her and fetched her sweater off the floor. Although I was disappointed to see her sweet curves disappear behind her fluffy sweater, she was so freaking cute in it, and I loved that too.

"I'll get the door," I offered as she shimmied off the counter.

I strode to the sink and washed my hands quickly, snagging a paper towel as I crossed toward the living room. I gave the pizza driver a generous tip because it was snowing like crazy outside. Although I'd plowed Mae's drive just over an hour ago, several more inches had already collected.

"Road's okay?" I asked the driver over the swirling wind.

"Of course, man, I'm getting tips like mad," the guy replied with a lopsided grin.

"Be safe!" I called as he dashed back to his car.

When I returned to the kitchen, Mae announced, "I'll get our dinner when we go out."

My palm was warm where it rested on the bottom

of the box of pizza. "Oh, so that means we're getting dinner together?"

"Yes." Her lips twitched in barely a smile, and I savored the tinge of pink on her cheeks.

While she got plates out, my memory spun back to our three kisses in college. Only three, and they'd been that memorable. Those memories felt different and distant now. Everything I was feeling now was something I hadn't felt before. I wanted to take care of her, to wipe away those lingering worries that flitted through her eyes again and again.

We had pizza and watched another episode of *Schitt's Creek*. After we finished eating, she opened the front door and peered out. Turning back, she announced, "You can't drive home."

"I can drive home," I insisted even though I wanted to stay the night. "Mae, it's not a big deal. I'm three driveways down. I can handle it."

The thing was, if I stayed here, I wouldn't be able to stop kissing her. I didn't know how I knew, but I knew I couldn't rush it with her.

She fussed and even told me to zip my jacket. I remote started my SUV and then looked down at her. "So when are we having dinner?"

"Friday or Saturday?" she returned. Before I could answer, she added, "Saturday. I might be tired Friday because I have to go into Anchorage every Friday."

"Well, we don't want you tired," I teased. She rolled her eyes. "Saturday it is. Give me your number."

She looked at me for a long moment. "It's the same number I had before. Do you have the same number?"

It had been years, but I did have the same phone number. I slid my phone out of my pocket and pulled up my contacts, scrolling through. My lips curled into a slow smile when I saw her name. Mae T. was all it said.

"It's Townsend," she said.

I eyed her. "I know that. Do you still have my number on your phone?"

Her cheeks flushed pink, and she turned, snatching her phone off the coffee table. She walked back to me and then looked up with a sheepish smile. "I don't. I probably deleted it."

"Ah, something like that," I said lightly, ignoring the sting on my heart. "Here, I'll text you."

As soon as the text went through, she tapped it open and added my number to her contacts.

"One more thing," I said.

"What?" Her lashes lifted, and her eyes met mine.

"Another kiss," I murmured as I bent low and slid my hand into her hair.

I meant for it to be brief, but apparently, I couldn't kiss Mae without it getting hot, *fast*. The next thing I knew, we were breathless, and I was about to spin her against the door when I caught myself. I lifted my head with a low laugh.

MAE

I drummed my fingertips against my thigh as I waited in line at Firehouse Café. I'd missed this place, and I hadn't known how much until I came home. I looked around, absorbing the familiar space. The artwork on the walls had changed because Janet rotated artwork from Alaskan artists, but fireweed was still painted on the old fire pole. The brightly painted chairs and tables added a cheery vibe to the space, and the same chalkboard menu hung on the wall behind the counter, though probably with some updates. The best part was getting to the front of the line and being greeted with one of Janet's warm smiles. Her hair had more silver in it than before, but her smile was just as wide.

"Hey, girl."

"Hey, Janet."

"It's good to see you here a few times a week," she added, her eyes crinkling at the corners with her smile.

"It's good to be here a few times a week."

"Your usual?"

"Yes, ma'am."

She quickly prepped my favorite dark mocha with

no sugar. "How's your job?" she asked as she counted out change for me, which I promptly stuffed in her tip jar.

"I love it so far."

"Your parents are mighty happy you're back."

I smiled. "And I'm glad to be here."

"Don't be a stranger," she said.

"Have I been a stranger?" I turned back.

"Absolutely not. Just making sure it stays that way," she teased before shifting her attention to the customers behind me.

I crossed over to snag the only table left by the windows, smiling as I looked out on Main Street. A layer of snow dusted the signs and rooftops, and Christmas decorations were up on storefronts. I took a deep breath and let it out, a sense of relaxation I hadn't felt in years sliding through me. It was good to be home. I'd always meant to get back to Alaska, but I hadn't known when it would happen.

I wondered what Rowan thought of Willow Brook now that he lived here. My thoughts were playing a game of ping pong around him. Every time I mentally shifted to another topic, my thoughts bounced right back to him. Fortunately, I'd moved on from my annoyance at his presence. Gah! The other night had been crazy hot. Except now I had a new worry.

I was going to have to tell him what really happened and explain all my hang-ups around trust and everything else. Before I could get stuck in anxiety quicksand, someone called my name. I glanced over to see Holly and Ella waving from the line.

"Hey!" I called over.

There was one chair across from me and an empty one at a table nearby. "Can I snag that chair?" I asked the older couple sitting there.

"It's all yours," the woman replied with a smile.

I grabbed it before someone else could, and a few minutes later, Holly flounced in the chair across from me with Ella right on her heels. I leaned over and gave Ella a quick hug. "I haven't seen you in weeks."

"You've only been here a few weeks," Ella returned with a grin.

"I know, but it's just good to see everyone."

"I don't have much of a social life. Having a baby kind of absorbs everything."

"Yeah?"

Ella nodded, her glossy brown hair swinging with the motion. "Babies mean hardly any sleep. But I don't want to be *that* friend, the one whose non-baby friends can't stand."

Holly rolled her eyes. "That's not gonna happen."

Ella nudged her knee against Holly's before she looked back toward me. "So, how's life? You're all settled in?"

"I am. I like my job. Gram's house is great. I do need to redecorate, kind of desperately, though. I feel like I'm living in a time warp. I should have disco parties."

After laughing about that, Holly decided we'd plan a day trip to Anchorage to pick out paint and something to replace the shag carpet. After catching up a little bit more, Ella had to leave.

She stood from the table, leaning over and dusting a kiss on my cheek. "I'm so glad you're back. We'll see each other soon."

After she left, I glanced over at Holly. "What's your schedule today?"

Her eyes bounced to the clock above the door. "I have to get to work in an hour. Until then, I'm hanging with you."

"What if I have plans?" I teased.

Holly's brown eyes twinkled with her smile. "So, tell me the update on you and Rowan."

"What do you mean?" I hedged.

"Don't play coy. I saw him kiss you the other night."

Instantly, my neck got hot. I bought myself a moment by finishing my cup of coffee. "What do you mean?" I finally countered.

Holly cocked her head to the side. "In the parking lot at the pizza place," she replied pointedly.

"Oh, right." For a split second, I thought I would try to play it cool, but Holly was my friend, and I needed a friend.

I rested my elbows on the table and leaned my face into my hands as I let out a sigh. Brushing my hair back from my face, I lifted my eyes to hers again. "I don't know what to do."

Holly's teasing gaze faded. "What happened?"

"He stopped by last night and helped me with the driveway because I couldn't start the plow truck. We, um, kissed again." It wasn't just my neck now. My face felt like it was on fire.

"Was it more than a kiss?" Holly leaned forward.

"Yes, but I don't know what to do." Ugh. I didn't even know how to explain it.

"What happened with you two before?"

"I told you. I met him at UNC, we were friends for a while, then we went on a few dates, and then—" My words came to an abrupt halt, while my thoughts scattered. I knew what this was. The therapist I'd seen had helped me understand how my brain tried to protect itself by avoiding the traumatic memories. But that didn't help in the long run because then I never learned to face them.

Holly watched me quietly before prompting, "Let's not worry about the past. Do you like him now?"

There was a big fat black hole in my past that I didn't want to explore, most definitely not now in a coffee shop, so I was grateful she sensed that somehow. "Well, obviously, but—" I groaned. "I don't know."

"Do you know if you like him or not?"

"I know I like him."

I worried the corner of my bottom lip as I considered being honest with her. I knew I could trust Holly. "Can I tell you something?"

"Anything, you know I'm a vault."

"I—" I tried to force the words out, but they were stuck.

Holly waited patiently. "Here, I'll tell you something."

"Uh, okay?"

She shrugged lightly. "You seem embarrassed about it, so I'll tell you my embarrassing thing."

Embarrassment was part of my messy feelings, but just the tip of it. But I was curious now. "Okay, what?"

"I was a virgin until Nate."

"What?" I squeaked, genuinely surprised.

She flushed slightly. "I was almost thirty. Nobody knew, well, except for Nate. I wasn't saving myself for someone either, and it just turned into this *thing*."

"What do you mean?"

Holly shrugged. "You know in high school, there was everything that happened with Jake."

"I know. That was—" I paused, unsure how to describe it.

"Awful, sad, disruptive," Holly offered helpfully with a twist of her lips.

Holly and Ella, along with Ella's now-husband

Caleb and Holly's boyfriend, were in a car accident on an icy patch of Turnagain Arm, a highway that led out of Anchorage along a winding stretch by the mountains. They'd been hit by a drunk driver, and Holly's boyfriend had died instantly when he was thrown from the vehicle. That accident had been defining for a lot of us in high school, most obviously for Holly, Caleb, and Ella. Caleb and Ella had broken up at the time. I was glad they were back together because they'd been one of those couples I'd thought were going to make it.

"It was terrible and so sad," I offered somberly.

"It just fucked so many things up. Jake and I weren't like Caleb and Ella. I mean, we were together and I liked him, but then he died, and it just messed everything up. You try dating in this town after something like that happens. Everyone treats you like you're tragic," she said dryly.

"Oh, god, I never really thought about that."

"Yeah, and I couldn't talk about it. Like, my boyfriend died, and nobody wanted to touch me. So, there was that, and then college and just life. Before I knew it, I was staring down thirty and wondering how long I'd be stuck a virgin."

I chuckled. "You used to hate Nate."

Holly rolled her eyes and laughed. "I know. I mean, he was Alex's best friend, still is. I still can't believe we're together sometimes."

"I'm really happy for you two."

Holly smiled before her gaze sobered. "So, whatever you're not sure you can tell me, no judgment from me. And, whatever it is, you should just tell Rowan. Secrets mess everything up."

My stomach flipped at the mere thought of telling Rowan. "What do you know about him?"

"Probably less than you," Holly offered.

"Has he dated anybody since he's been in town?"

"Not that I know of," Holly said, scrunching up her nose thoughtfully. "I would hear about it. Between Nate flying for the hotshot crews in the summer and knowing everybody on those crews, I'd know. He hasn't dated anybody. You can't really hide your social life in Willow Brook, even if you try. Trust me, I tried."

I laughed. "Well, I guess we're going to dinner next weekend."

"Oh, like a date?" Her tone was low and teasing.

"I guess."

"Where are you going to have dinner?"

"I don't know." I was seriously doubting whether dinner with Rowan was a smart plan.

"You'd better just go to Anchorage unless you want everyone in town to gossip about you," she offered helpfully.

"I know, but I don't want to drive to Anchorage on the weekend. That's like a *thing*."

Holly shrugged. "You could always do a Firehouse dinner. That's less of a social place at night than Wildlands. There's that restaurant beside the gallery."

"Oh, right, what's the deal with the gallery?"

"Jasmine manages it. I've heard the restaurant's good, but I haven't eaten there. It's only been open for like three weeks. It's as fresh as you being back," she teased.

We were laughing when I heard the bell jingle above the door and reflexively glanced over to see Rowan walking in. The second my eyes landed on him, heat raced through me, my skin prickling with awareness. I didn't know how he knew I was sitting over here, but his eyes swung straight toward me. It felt as if a line connected us across the room—a shimmering, sparking line. I could feel the burn.

"Whoa," Holly whispered.

"Shut up," I hissed, whipping my eyes away from Rowan.

She grinned unabashedly. "That is one hot look from him. He's pretty hot too, all dark and quiet."

"I know," I returned with a sigh. "It doesn't help matters."

"Well, I need to get to work." Holly leaned back, sliding her arms into her jacket.

"You said you didn't have to be back to work for an hour," I protested.

"I lied." She stood, resting her hand on my shoulder and giving it a quick squeeze. "I'm so glad you're back." She blew me a kiss and hurried out.

I told myself to stand and leave, but I couldn't make myself do it. As I was watching her walk away, Rowan turned my way. My belly swooped, and my pulse raced off like a horse set loose in a pasture.

I watched as he walked over, my eyes tracking his easy stride. His down jacket was unzipped, and he wore a T-shirt underneath. I knew just how hard and muscled his chest was. My eyes landed on the sharp chiseled line of his jaw before lingering on his slightly crooked lips. He stopped by the table, and I stared up at him, the rush of blood in my ears making it hard to think.

"Hey there, Mae," he said, his honeyed drawl sliding over me.

"Hey," I managed a little breathlessly.

"Mind if I join you?"

"Of course not."

He sat down across from me, stretching one leg out. "How are you?" he asked.

I nodded in response, and one of his dark brows rose. "What?" I prompted.

"I don't know what a nod means as to how you are." His lips twitched, and my belly fluttered.

"Oh, I'm good. How are you?" I returned, feeling too flustered with the whole thing. Dear God, I couldn't even manage polite conversation with him.

"Better."

"Better?"

"Seeing you makes my morning better," he said simply.

Oh. My. God. This man could really ruin me. When he looked at me, I felt encompassed by his full attention. His gaze alone was like an embrace, hot and unsettling while also comforting and patient.

"Tell me where we should have dinner," I blurted out.

He shrugged. "Wherever you want."

"Holly just told me there's a new restaurant beside the new gallery."

Rowan's lips curled in a slow smile, and my belly dipped again. "I don't know what it's called, but let's go."

"Or should we head to Anchorage?" I was shaking my head at my own question.

"If you want to go to Anchorage, we can go to Anchorage," he said easily.

I shook my head again.

"I want whatever you want, sugar," he replied.

Gah! Rowan and his endearments.

We were sitting there quietly when someone cleared their throat. I glanced up to discover Janet standing there with a tray resting on her arm. Her eyes twinkled as she smiled at us.

"All done with your coffee?"

"Yes." I handed her my mug, and she set it on the tray.

"I know you're not done yet, but you have a to-go cup," she said to Rowan.

"I do." He winked.

Janet's eyes were warm as she looked back at me. "He's a charmer, and he has excellent manners." She squeezed his shoulder lightly. "You be good to Mae."

"Always," he replied, the teasing look in his eyes fading to somber.

Janet winked before she hurried away to gather plates at the next table. Feeling befuddled, I looked back over at Rowan. I could have sworn his green eyes darkened. After a moment, he said, "Unfortunately, I have to get to the station soon."

He stood, hesitating beside my chair and startling me out of my wits when he leaned down and brushed his lips across mine. "I couldn't resist," he murmured as he straightened.

I watched him walk out of the café with my lips tingling and electricity pinging through my body like a pinball machine.

Chapter Twelve

ROWAN

"What's with you and Mae?" Russell asked.

Glancing toward him while I rubbed my damp hair with a towel, I countered with, "What do you mean?"

Russell's eyes took on a glint with his sly grin. "Dude, this town's the size of a thimble. I was at Firehouse this morning when you kissed her before you left. You didn't even notice Paisley and me standing in line."

I cast a sheepish smile his way. "Fair enough. How are things with you and Paisley?"

Russell and Paisley were pretty fresh as a couple. Paisley had been on our crew, but she'd switched to another crew after Russell fessed up that he was in love with her. He'd tried to persuade Graham to switch her back, but she held her ground. I liked Paisley, and I thought she was good for Russell. I hadn't even known the guy that long.

"We're good. How do you know Mae?" he countered, not letting me change the subject.

"We knew each other in college."

"Ah. I've known Mae as long as I can remember," he added.

"Oh, of course. You both grew up here."

"Did you date her in college?" he prompted as he tossed a towel in the laundry basket in the corner and tugged on a pair of jeans over his briefs.

"We went on a few dates," I offered, hoping to keep it vague.

Russell buttoned his jeans and glanced up, his gaze sharpening. "What the hell happened?"

At that moment, Graham, our superintendent, came walking in from the showers. "What did happen?" he interjected.

"Oh, my god," I muttered under my breath.

Graham clapped me on the shoulder with a chuckle. "I don't even know what you guys are talking about."

I snagged a clean T-shirt out of my bag and pulled it over my head just as Russell explained, "Rowan's got a thing with Mae, and they used to date."

"I didn't know you were so nosy." I shook my head as I glanced over at him.

"I'm only nosy about my friends."

"We were good friends and went on a few dates. Her roommate hit on me when I was at a party. I still don't know what else happened, but after that, Mae stopped talking to me."

"Oh," Graham said, looking suitably horrified. "Mae's really nice."

I sighed. "I know. I didn't do anything with her roommate. I swear."

Russell chuckled. "Does she hate you? Because Paisley hated me. You can work through that," he offered helpfully.

Graham toweled off and started getting dressed.

"She must not hate him that much. I already heard that he kissed her at Firehouse this morning."

I groaned. I couldn't believe I was fucking explaining this shit. "I think she might have sort of hated me, but we're past that now. I never got on her nerves the way you did Paisley's."

Russell shrugged nonchalantly. "Hey, it's good for some things."

"And *that* is all I needed to hear about that," Graham said dryly. He stood and stuffed his feet into a pair of winter boots.

"You're not her boss anymore," Russell added.

"Nope. And I think it's best for both of you that you're not on the same crew anymore."

"Why, though? I like being on the same schedule as her," Russell pressed.

"Because there's a reason Ward and Susanna aren't on the same crew. You don't need to be worried about how she's doing out in the field," Graham said flatly.

Russell grumbled before nodding. "I get it, even if I don't like it. I gotta bolt," he said as he put his jacket on. "You be good to Mae." He pointed at me before he strode out of the room.

I shrugged into my jacket and checked my locker to make sure I had my keys. When I turned, I collided with Graham's assessing gaze. I liked him as superintendent for the crew. He was solid, had no tolerance for drama, and he treated everyone on the crew as equals.

"How well do you know Mae?" I heard myself asking, immediately cursing myself.

"She was a year or two behind me in school, but we grew up together in Willow Brook," Graham offered. "Her parents are good people."

My gaze whipped to his. Because I was *that* fucking

hungry for information about Mae. "To my knowledge, she's never been serious with anybody. At least not here. Her mom's friends with my mom, and I hear everything from my mom because she's a gossip. According to my mom and her mom, she's never had a serious relationship."

"So, this is like fourth hand?" I asked dryly.

Graham chuckled. "My mom thinks she has baggage."

"How the hell does your mom know that?"

"Small fucking town, dude. Like I said, her mom and my mom are practically besties."

I took a breath, letting it out quickly. "I wish I'd been a few years older when I knew her before. Maybe then, I'd have had enough sense to figure out what the hell went wrong."

"I get it, man. I know all about being too young to know better. I got a daughter from it. Best thing that ever happened to me. No judgment on that score. Just —" He paused, studying me for a beat. "Mae's not the kind of girl to play casual with. I don't know you that well because you've only been around for a few months, but you seem solid. You don't seem like the kind of guy who'd fuck with her feelings."

"I'm not," I said solemnly.

It wasn't like I was planning to marry Mae all of a sudden, but I would never play with her feelings. I didn't want to hurt her, by accident or otherwise. I suspected something I'd done before had hurt her by accident.

"You want to grab a beer?" Graham asked.

"Sure."

I could use a beer, and I liked hanging out with Graham. I liked most of the guys on my crew.

Phoebe happened to be walking past our locker room, and Graham called out, "Yo, Phoebe!"

She stopped, leaning around the doorway to peer into the locker room. "What's up, guys?"

"Crew night at Wildlands," Graham replied.

"Who's going?"

"Just us three," he returned.

"And me," a voice chimed in when Chase appeared beside her.

"All right, let's do it," Phoebe replied, nudging Chase with her shoulder.

Chapter Thirteen

ROWAN

Wildlands was clearly a favorite hangout in town, and not just for the hotshot crews. "This place stays busy all the time," I commented as I glanced around the full restaurant and the crowded bar.

"Always," Graham agreed.

Phoebe lifted her beer and took a swallow. After setting it down, she let her gaze arc around the space before it came to me. "I remember when I was a kid. I couldn't wait to be old enough to come here when it was a bar. And now it's old news, and I'm not even thirty yet." She twisted her mouth to the side and let out a sigh.

Paisley slipped into a chair beside Phoebe at that moment, catching the tail end of her comment. "Thirty is not that old."

Phoebe's eyes slid to her, and she shrugged. "Maybe not, but I feel old right now."

Graham's brows hitched up. "Well, at least you don't have a fourteen-year-old daughter. She manages to make me feel fucking ancient sometimes."

I chuckled. "Makes sense. I have a sixteen-year-old sister, and she makes me feel ancient."

"Oh, you have a sister?" Phoebe commented.

"Oh, yeah. She was my parents' surprise baby, and apparently, now she's dating some asshole." I sighed and shook my head.

Graham's eyes widened. "I can't deal. I'll lose my shit if that happens with Allie."

"I'm hoping it's a short relationship."

A few others joined us, and it was nice to relax and hang out with friends from work. I knew the very second Mae walked in because I felt the hair rise on my forearms and a prickle of awareness run down my spine. I glanced over my shoulder. She was by herself and paused, glancing around as if she were looking for someone. As soon as her eyes landed on mine, I waved and stood. I heard Graham's snort, but I ignored it as I walked toward her.

"Looking for someone?" I asked when I stopped in front of her.

Her pretty ginger eyes met mine. "Holly's meeting me here." She pulled her phone out of her pocket and then sighed. "Oh, she canceled because she's staying late at work. Shit."

"Come sit with me."

"You sure?" A little crease formed between her eyes, and I wanted to smooth it away.

"Of course, I'm sure. I'm just hanging out with the crew, all of whom you probably know better than I do. Come on." I reached for her hand without thinking. The second I touched her, I thought she'd pull away, but she didn't, and the feel of her fingers lacing into mine felt just right.

When we reached the table, Phoebe had already scooted over and patted the chair beside her. "Hey,

Mae!" They side-hugged quickly, and Phoebe's curious eyes landed on mine. "You know Rowan then?"

A pink tinge bloomed on Mae's cheeks when she nodded. "I do." I was about to explain when Mae added, "We knew each other in college."

A server stopped by the table. After that, conversation flowed easily, and I watched while Mae caught up with the friends she'd grown up with. It was kind of strange because, to me, she took up so much space in my memory that it felt as if I'd known her forever. Yet she'd known many of these people much longer than me.

I was glad to see Mae, really glad. But there was one small problem—I couldn't be near her without being hyperaware of everything. Her knee brushed mine at one point. Just that subtle touch was so hot, it was as if I'd been singed by a flame. I had to adjust the way I was sitting because my arousal was tight in the confines of my jeans.

Fuck me. Mae was a straight shot into the vein of my desire. She was hungry and ordered food, but eschewed a glass of wine because she was driving. An hour or more later, I realized I could hardly focus on the conversation around me.

While Mae was chatting with Phoebe about something, Graham nudged me with his elbow. "Dude, you're pathetic."

"What do you mean?" I glanced at him.

"You've got it bad."

I didn't even try to deny it. "I know."

Eventually, the group filtered apart, and I walked out with Mae, reaching for her hand while we walked down the narrow hallway in the back. I held her hand all the way out to her car. She tapped the key fob to start it before looking up at me. "You can go, you know. I can drive myself home," she said lightly.

"I know you can. Just one thing."

"What's that?" Her breath puffed in the cold air.

I rested my hands on her car, caging her between my arms. She smiled up at me, her eyes searching mine.

I wanted to take her home so bad and have her all to myself. But I knew I needed to take it slow, so I told myself a kiss would be okay. Actually, a kiss would be fucking amazing. I knew what it was like to kiss Mae.

She had on this cute little knit cap with her hair tucked underneath. "I like this," I said, running my fingertips along the edge of the stitching.

"I knitted it myself."

"Did you now?"

She nodded. "I like to knit."

"What would I have to do to get you to knit me one of these?"

Her lips twitched, and a giggle slipped out. "I don't know. I'll have to think about it."

"How about a kiss?" I murmured when my lips were but a whisper away from hers.

"How about this?"

She leaned up, brushing her lips across mine. The second her tongue darted out, I let out something between a growl and a groan. Once again, we tumbled into kiss after kiss, and I took deep sips from her mouth.

Before I knew it, I had her plastered against me. I even forgot where we were until the sound of a door slamming and a horn honking snapped me into awareness. I lifted my head, taking in a gulp of the icy cold air.

Her forehead dropped to my chest. "We can't seem to just kiss, huh?"

A laugh rustled in my throat. "Right now, that's all that's happening. You're going to get in that car, and you're going to go home. I'm going to see you for dinner next."

She lifted her head and peered up at me. "I need to tell you something." She was suddenly serious, but she also looked nervous.

"Okay, you can tell me anything."

"Stupid, stupid, stupid," I muttered to myself.

Rowan had waited for me to explain what the hell I meant to tell him, and then I freaked and said I had to go. I hadn't even given him a chance to stop me, fumbling and dropping my keys before I could get in my car. He'd sent me a text, asking if we could talk, and I hadn't replied yet.

I was in the bathtub at the house. Gram had a great bathtub—an old clawfoot tub, extra deep with the perfect angle to rest my head against the back. I felt so keyed up over telling him I needed to tell him something. I couldn't even relax. Now I was going to have to cancel dinner. Ugh.

After I toweled off and dressed in my most comfortable pajamas, I plunked down on the couch with a bowl of popcorn. I turned on *Schitt's Creek* because I needed something to lighten my mood. I'd even been avoiding looking at my phone out of fear he would text me again. I finally got up the nerve to look at the screen.

Rowan: *So you kind of freaked out there. I don't know*

what you need to tell me, but for God's sake, don't cancel dinner on me.

Before I could think better of it, I responded.

Me: *It's nothing you want to know, so can we forget I said I needed to tell you something.*

I hit send, jabbing at my phone screen.

His reply was swift.

Rowan: *Mae, I can't forget that you said that. Just tell me. Can I call you?*

Me: *Not now. I don't want to talk about it. I am canceling dinner. You can't tell me I can't cancel.*

Rowan: *Can I please come over? I'd rather not try to have this convo over text.*

Before I could reply, my phone rang in my hand. I stared at his number as it flashed, then reluctantly swiped my thumb across the screen.

"What?" I knew my tone sounded mulish, but I didn't care. I was doing all I could to keep from panicking. Rowan didn't need to know anything about that night.

"Can we rewind?"

"Sure. I have nothing to tell you."

"Mae, please don't do this. I know you're not telling me something about why you stopped talking to me. You have to know it's been driving me crazy. Whatever it is, just tell me."

My heart raced, and I felt a little sick. My skin felt tingly but not in a good way. I was so relieved Rowan couldn't see me.

"Let's just have dinner," he prompted.

"Okay, fine," I muttered.

I was about to hang up when Rowan's voice caught me like a hook. "You mean a lot to me, Mae."

"Huh?"

"I don't know what went wrong and why you

stopped talking to me, but I was half in love with you in college. If it was your roommate hitting on me, just tell me so I know. I hate that I didn't have a chance to figure out what happened. All these years, I thought you kind of hated me."

My heart twisted in my chest. "I didn't hate you, Rowan," I whispered.

"Okay, well, I just wanted you to know you mean a lot to me," he said in his slow Southern drawl.

My belly was all fluttery, and I felt as if I were a stick of butter melting in the hot sun. This man was treacherous for my heart. I didn't let myself get vulnerable for a reason, and now it was happening with him in spite of all of my defenses.

Maybe it will be okay. Maybe if you tell Rowan the whole truth, it won't blow up in your face.

My hopeful little heart whispered to me, and I wanted to ignore it. But it was hard, so very hard, to resist Rowan and my feelings for him. All this time, I'd thought if I could block out everything and everyone who reminded me of the worst night of my life, I could forget it. Even though my therapist had gently and carefully tried to help me face the fact that I couldn't just erase my own memory.

"So, dinner Saturday at that new gallery restaurant? Tell me what time I'm picking you up," he prompted.

"Oh, so you're picking me up?"

The sound of his low chuckle sent shivers chasing over my skin. "I'd like to."

Against all reason, I gave in. Dinner wouldn't hurt me. "Okay. Five thirty. It gets dark early, so I don't like to be out late."

"Five thirty, it is. Good night, Mae."

I lay in bed staring at the ceiling with an elbow propped behind my head and my other palm resting flat on the mattress. I couldn't stop thinking about Mae.

Realizing I wasn't going to sleep unless I took matters into my own hand, literally, I reached down and slid my hand over my arousal. I let out a groan, recalling the feel of Mae's lips underneath mine. Only moments later, my release spurted over my belly. I let out a ragged sigh. Maybe I'd sleep now.

Fuck. What the hell wasn't Mae telling me?

After cleaning up in the bathroom and returning to my bed, I punched my pillow under my head as I rolled onto my side. I'd been thinking we would finally let this bonfire burn like flames into the sky. But now, I thought it was best if I took things even more slowly.

Phoebe sat across from me at Firehouse Café, blinking back tears.

"Oh, wow. That's really shitty," I said.

She lifted her cup of coffee and took a quick swallow before setting it down with a thump. "I know. Trust me, I know."

"You and Tasha were like best friends in high school."

"Sure were."

"Oh, god. And the wedding's going to be here in town?" I asked slowly.

"Yep."

"Well, none of us are going to stand up for Tasha. I don't care who she asks," I said firmly.

Phoebe had just broken the news that her high school best friend was engaged to her ex-fiancé. Apparently, right after they had broken up this summer, Phoebe walked in on her friend and her ex. Now, they were already getting married and planning a wedding here in this tiny town.

"Maybe your mom should talk to the pastor or

their friends. Maybe they won't even hold the wedding here."

Phoebe rolled her eyes. "You know they will."

"Tell me what happened."

"Dirk and I broke up before I found out. I didn't want to marry him, and I don't want him back. It's just —" She let out a frustrated sigh. "Fuck. It feels like being emotionally dropkicked. She was my best friend. Who does that? I found out after the fact that they'd been screwing around for months behind my back, and now they're getting married."

"How did you find out they were getting married?"

"Tasha called to beg for my forgiveness, and she wants me to be there. She feels like she needs to close the loop and heal the circle or some bullshit. You don't fuck your friend's fiancé behind their back. That's like a rule, right?"

"Yep, that is *definitely* a rule in the unwritten friendship handbook," I said firmly.

Phoebe knuckled at a tear that escaped and slipped down her cheek. I stood, rounding the table to give her a quick hug. "She's a shitty friend."

Phoebe gave me a hard squeeze in return, and I returned to my chair across from her.

"I know she is. It's just I really don't want to deal with having it thrown in my face here in town."

"Honestly, I'm a little shocked she's having the wedding here," I commented, breaking off a piece of my scone and popping it in my mouth.

My friend twisted her lips to the side as she rolled her eyes. "I know, right? It's fucked up."

"For what it's worth, you always had more friends than Tasha did." I was feeling a little petty, but it was true.

Phoebe laughed. "I guess so."

"How can I help?"

Phoebe cast me a quick smile. "You already did. Do I have to forgive her?"

"Maybe for your own sanity, but forgiveness doesn't mean you have to be her friend again. Nobody would expect that."

Phoebe stared at me quietly, her brow knitting. "What do you mean?"

"Just that. I'm not saying right this second you need to forgive Tasha for screwing around with your fiancé. Even if you didn't want to stay with him, that is off-limits for anyone who claims to be a friend. What I mean is you can let it go when you're ready, but that doesn't mean you have to be her best friend again."

She studied me for a moment before cocking her head to the side. "I think that's what she wants. She says she misses our friendship."

"Yeah, well, she doesn't get to define how your forgiveness looks. Letting go is healthy for everyone." In defiance of my own words, I silently shrugged inside. I wasn't sure I could ever forgive one person—Chet. He had a shitty name, but I knew letting go might be healthy for me.

"That helps me think about it. I don't think I'm there yet with the forgiveness," she said honestly.

"Well, you don't have to be. It's pretty freaking fresh, and she's got some nerve. You know what we should do?"

"What?"

"We should book up everything in town so she can't find anywhere to hold her reception. I doubt the pastor will refuse to do the wedding, but we can make the rest difficult for her," I offered with a sly grin.

Phoebe laughed softly. "I'll deal. The less I think

about it, the better. On another note, you know who's moving back to town?"

"Aside from me?" I teased.

"Yeah, aside from you, although that's news, and I'm glad you're here."

"Who?"

"Archer Cannon."

I rifled through my memories. "Archer from elementary school? The kid you hung out with all the time?" At her nod, I asked, "Didn't he move away before we even got to high school?"

"Yup. He was my best friend back when we were little."

"I remember. He was getting kind of cute before he moved. Maybe you guys can have a fling?"

Phoebe's eyes widened comically. "Um, Archer wasn't that kind of friend."

"It was elementary school," I countered.

She burst out laughing. "True. Like, no guy is hot in the fifth grade."

We laughed again, and I was grateful for something to focus on other than my own worries.

Chapter Seventeen

ROWAN

I had sent a quick email to my old friend Darryl, asking if he knew anything I didn't about what might've happened with Mae. If there was anything to know, he might know it. Ever since Mae had said she needed to tell me something, something was niggling in my thoughts. I chalked it up to me being upset with Mae back then for cutting me out without explanation.

After she stopped talking to me, biology lab had been tense for the rest of that semester. After that, we didn't have any classes together.

Opening my email, I was surprised to see his reply only a day later. "Call me. I think I know what you're asking about."

Scrolling through my contacts, I found his old number. "Hey, man," he said as soon as he answered. "How the hell are you?"

"Pretty good. Life's busy. How about you? You still working in law?"

"Of course. It's kind of dry, but I actually like it. Got married. About to have our second kid."

"Good for you, man. That's what you wanted, right?" Darryl had been a solid friend who knew what he wanted—a steady job with decent money and a family. The guy kept it simple.

"Good thing it's what I wanted. I love kids. They're hysterical and messy. What about you? You were doing the firefighter thing last I knew," he replied.

"Still am. I'm out in Alaska. A buddy from my hometown who's also a firefighter told me about an opening out here, so I jumped on it."

"Ah, you do love to travel. How is Alaska? What's it like?"

"Fucking gorgeous and kind of mind-blowing. There are moose everywhere."

Darryl chuckled. "So that's not an exaggeration?"

"Nope. Anyway, you said for me to call you."

"I did. You sure you want to know? I thought you knew, or I'd have told you."

My gut turned over. "What is it?"

"It was that night you couldn't find Mae at that party. You remember Chet?"

"Yeah. Hard to forget that asshole." At the mere mention of Chet's name, dread coated my stomach with a bitter acid.

Chet was a fucking dick, the worst kind of guy. He'd only been our roommate for that one year. We'd chosen not to renew a lease because we didn't want him there anymore.

"What happened?" I prompted.

"I don't know all the details, but I'm pretty sure he spiked her drink. Steph heard about it," he explained, referring to his wife, who'd been his girlfriend back then.

My heart seized and then lunged into a pounding

beat. After Chet moved out, rumors traveled about him spiking women's drinks with a date rape drug and then raping them and claiming it was consensual. We didn't find out about this level of his assfuckery until after he moved out.

"Oh, my fucking god."

"I know. Even though they were just rumors, I always wondered if they were true. He was a next-level asshole."

"Fuck. I know. Darryl, you knew Mae. She wasn't a partier. He didn't usually go for that kind of girl." I was grasping at anything to somehow make this not true.

Oh, fuck, fuck, fuck, fuck, fuck. No, no, no!

I was standing in the kitchen in my apartment, and my knees felt a little wobbly. I walked over and plunked down on the couch.

"Chet didn't have a type. He just liked to take advantage if he thought he could," my friend said flatly.

"Oh, my god," I breathed. "No wonder she was so pissed off at me. Did you know that back then?"

"Fuck no! I'd have told you if I did. I found out because Stephanie heard from another one of the girls who knew Mae. I told her about your email, and that's what she told me. I'd like to think it was bullshit, but you know how Chet was."

"Oh, my god," I repeated. I was trying to wrap my brain around this hellish news.

"What brings this up now?"

"I'm in Alaska, and that's where Mae's from. It's kind of a weird coincidence, but when my friend told me where the job was, I wanted to take it because I hoped I could reconnect with her. She kind of fell off the radar."

"How is she?" he asked.

I took a shaky breath. "I'm not sure now. I mean, she's okay, but I didn't know this. I couldn't ever forget her. She's just, I don't know. You know how it is."

Darryl's laugh rustled through the line. "I do. That's why I married Stephanie."

I managed to laugh, but it was dry and tinged with bitterness. My laughter died in my throat. "Fuck," I muttered.

"Yeah, sorry to tell you that. It's awful."

"Should I tell Mae what I know?"

"Hell if I know. That's intense. I don't know."

"Can I talk to Stephanie?" I hadn't spoken to his wife in years, but I knew her from college because they started dating when I lived with Darryl. I was near frantic to talk to her.

"Right now?"

"Please, if you don't mind."

My friend moved the phone away from his mouth, calling, "Steph!"

A few seconds later, I heard him explaining that I wanted to talk to her and why.

"Here she is," he said.

"Hi, Rowan. Nice to hear from you," she said.

"Same. Look, I know this might be weird."

"It's definitely a tough conversation to start with," Stephanie said.

Her tone was warm, radiating empathy and reminding me precisely why Darryl fell for her.

"Can you fill me in on what you heard? Did Mae remember what happened?"

Just asking that question caused my stomach to twist painfully.

"She was in my dorm, and we were in the same circle of friends. Mae told us what happened with

Chet. She remembers because she came to in the middle of it."

"Oh, my fucking god," I whispered hoarsely. I wanted to throw up. "Was she okay?"

"Well, I mean, no. She was pretty freaked out about it. I don't think she dated again at all after that. According to her old roommate, who was just a shallow gossip, Mae was a virgin before that, so—"

"Oh, fuck. Are you fucking serious? Sorry," I added quickly.

"No need to apologize. Swear all you want. It's an awful situation," Stephanie said.

"Yeah, it is." My voice was thick, and my throat ached.

"What brought all this up?"

"Mae and I went out a few times. She shut me down after that, but we'd been really good friends before, and I didn't know what had happened. When I found out about a job in her hometown, I took it, hoping to reconnect."

"Aw, that's kind of sweet," Stephanie said.

"What's sweet?"

"That you never could forget her."

I leaned back into the couch, running a hand through my hair. "No, I couldn't. And now I don't know what to do. Should I tell her what I know now?"

Stephanie let out a heavy sigh. "I don't know, but I don't know how you can keep it a secret if you want to be her friend or more."

"Oh, god. This is bad."

"You're a good man, Rowan. You always were one of the nice guys."

"I try to be." It almost hurt to speak.

"You have no good choices, but I think you have to

tell her what you know. And if she hates you for it, you're just gonna have to live with it."

"Great advice," I said dryly, feeling helpless.

I'd wanted to know what happened, and now I wished I could forget.

Stephanie's voice was warm and understanding. "The truth will set you free, or something like that."

"Yeah. Well, how are you?"

"Doing pretty well, all things considered. Maybe you should sweep her off her feet or something. Show her there are good men in the world."

"There are plenty of good men in the world, but there are lots of assholes. Chet was the worst," I muttered, anger spinning into the distress and pain echoing inside.

"Yeah, he was. You guys gave up a sweet apartment just so he wouldn't be your roommate anymore."

"I know, right? It's fucking ridiculous, but that's how bad he was."

"Good luck with this, whatever happens. Can you do me a favor?" she asked.

"Sure."

"Tell me how she's doing. And if it works out okay, I want to know."

"You got it."

At that, she returned the phone to Darryl, who also wished me luck before we ended the call.

I set the phone on the coffee table, resting my elbows on my knees and tunneling my hands through my hair with a ragged sigh. This was a doozy.

I didn't know what to do. I knew that if I told Mae before we had dinner, we would never have dinner. I didn't want to bring it up at dinner. I was going to have to wing it. I honestly had no idea how I was going to tell her what I knew. I felt beyond awful.

Rowan was nervous, which seemed out of character. I was the anxious one, and he wasn't supposed to be nervous. For maybe the sixth time tonight since we sat down at the table, he slid his palms over the tops of his thighs. The brushing sound was subtle over the denim.

The Gallery Café was chic but relaxed. Artwork from the gallery decorated the walls. The space had a tall ceiling with windows looking out over a marshy field. Dusk was leaching the light away. The mountains were cast in pink and lavender, alpenglow against the inky blue sky.

I took a sip of my water and glanced around the restaurant. Wooden tables with colorful placemats and tablecloths filled the space. The décor was modern with a touch of whimsy.

When my gaze made its way back to Rowan, my question slipped out, "What's wrong?"

He cleared his throat. "What do you mean?"

I knew him well enough to know he was hedging.

"You're nervous or something. What's up? You're not usually like this."

His eyes closed, and he took a breath as he opened them. "Nothing."

"Okay, don't bullshit me." My belly felt funny, and uncertainty slid through me. "Just say what's wrong."

"Uh, now is not a good time," he returned.

As I studied him, I knew. I didn't know how I knew. But I knew he *knew*.

"How do you know?" My next question slipped out, my voice a little ragged on the edges as my heart thumped sickly inside my chest.

If there was one thing I was an expert at in life, it was tolerating this very feeling—this feeling of awfulness, of a secret that I hated, this feeling of knowing that it was mine to carry forever even as I labored to cast the weight off.

"Fuck." His voice was sharp. "I'm sorry."

"It's obviously not your fault," I said calmly, literally feeling as if metal walls were falling down around me, like scales on an armadillo.

"Why didn't you tell me then?" he whispered hoarsely.

I couldn't even look at him and stared down at the tablecloth, tracing my fingertips along the hem. "Because I didn't want to tell you. I don't want you to know now," I said, my voice perfectly controlled even though I felt cold inside.

I didn't want to, but I looked up. Rowan's intense green eyes searched my face before he dipped his chin slowly. "I know you don't. I'm sorry."

"How do you know? Tell me how you found out," I demanded.

For some reason, I really needed to know this part.

He took a breath, letting it out swiftly. "What

happened always bothered me, and I didn't even know what happened. All I knew is that we were friends, and I totally had a crush on you. We finally went out, and then your roommate hit on me, which fucking sucked. And then, I know that you know nothing ever happened."

I nodded because it was true. It's just because of what happened to me that night. I couldn't deal with facing anyone connected to Chet, and Rowan had been his roommate.

"Then you just stopped talking to me. And honestly, I couldn't forget you. I looked for you, but you just disappeared."

"I didn't disappear," I whispered, my heart feeling cracked open.

"Okay, maybe you didn't disappear, but you sure didn't make it easy to find you. You never answered my texts, you never answered my emails, you never answered my calls. And then, when this job opened up out here, I thought maybe we could reconnect, and I could finally figure out what the hell I did wrong."

I couldn't lie to myself. It was bittersweet realizing that I'd meant as much to him as he had to me. Sometimes, things happen that ruin everything. The debris field left behind is so big that it encompasses other events and people, and everything gets destroyed. That's what happened to Rowan and me.

He stared at me quietly. "I would never hurt you."

My heart thumped painfully. I couldn't protect myself from my emotions. I took a gulp of icy water, clinging to the cold glass as if it would somehow get me through this.

Rowan continued, "I wasn't going to say this tonight here at dinner because obviously this isn't a good place."

I rolled my eyes, calling on some kind of composure to help me keep it together. Somehow, the shields around my heart held.

"I reached out to Darryl. I knew something weird had happened, but I just didn't know what. And, you know, he's married to Stephanie."

Ah, so that's how he found out. Stephanie knew. "So, they're still together?" I asked because that was a safe topic.

He nodded, his lips moving into the form of a smile, but it didn't reach his eyes. "Happily married. I guess they already have one kid, about to have the next."

Another sip of water. "Good for them. They were a good couple."

"I would never hurt you, Mae. I'm so sorry." His voice was hoarse, and I could feel the sense of helplessness emanating from him. Rowan liked to fix things, to take care of things. He couldn't fix this.

"I know, Rowan. You're the best kind of guy. It's just—" I waved my hand in the air because I didn't even know how to explain it, and the feelings that kind of got stuck on him. It was like when tires burned on the pavement.

"I'm really sorry."

"Stop apologizing for something you had nothing to do with."

"Why did you stop talking to me? I would've helped you. I would've fucking kicked his ass."

My chest ached, and emotion was knotted painfully in my throat. "You were a domino in the series of events. If I'd never been at the party, it never would've happened. I just wanted to forget everybody connected to him." I couldn't even say Chet's name out loud. Not now. I feared if I did, I'd fall apart right here.

"What about now?" he asked.

"I wouldn't be having dinner with you if you were still a domino in my mind."

"I was in love with you. I still am," he said, his tone completely serious.

I had just taken a swallow of water and almost spat it out. "What?" I yelped after I grabbed a napkin and dabbed at the table and my mouth.

His gaze was solemn as he stared at me. "It's true."

"Oh. Well, that sucks."

"It sucks?" A tiny smile lifted the corners of his mouth. At my nod, he added, "I kept texting and calling, and then I stopped because I didn't want to be stalkery."

"Stalkery? Is that a word."

"For the moment, it works." I couldn't look away from his eyes even though it hurt.

My heart felt as if someone had scored it deeply with a knife. My defenses cracked. It felt as if a hair-line fracture was somewhere in my psyche. In all of the defenses I'd built, Rowan was the fracture, or rather Rowan knowing what happened was.

"I just have one question," he said.

"Just one?"

"Okay, maybe more, but one for now." When I nodded, he asked, "Did you care as much as I did and still do?"

Oh, hell. I didn't know if I could hold my tears at bay. I closed my eyes and took a breath before I nodded, just once, really fast. Opening them, I collided instantly with his patient gaze. "I don't know if I knew I was in love with you, but you were *that* guy, the one I really wanted it to be okay with."

It was taking a lot of effort to keep those defenses up, but I managed because we were at a restaurant. I was actually relieved when the server showed up. She was in a hurry because the place was crowded. "Hi, how are we doing on the menu?"

Rowan's eyes held mine. I could tell he was waiting to see if I wanted more time. I didn't. I really needed to order some food. Even if I didn't think I could eat, I needed something to do with my hands.

"I'm ready," I said, my voice coming out a little forced.

She whipped out a little computer tablet. "What will it be?"

"Didn't you mention a special? Something with a glazed salmon?" I asked.

"Yes, we have salmon with a maple glaze and roasted on a cedar plank that comes with risotto and asparagus."

"Sounds perfect."

I didn't even hear what Rowan ordered, but then he asked, "Did you want to share that appetizer?"

"Which one?" I asked blankly.

My mind had derailed into the horror of what this dinner date had turned into.

"The fondue? You used to love fondue."

He smiled just a little bit, and my heart turned over in my chest. I wanted to cry. All the while, joy rose through the tangle of my emotions inside. When we'd first become friends before we'd actually dated in college, we'd bonded over our shared love of fondue at a little café that served it.

"Yes, I'll share."

He looked back up at the server. "That'll do it. Did you want anything other than water to drink?" she asked, glancing back and forth between us.

"I'll take a glass of the house wine," I said quickly.

"I'll take a beer, whatever the house draft is," Rowan added.

She hurried off, and then we were alone again. Even though we were in a busy restaurant surrounded by a low hum of voices, it truly felt as if we were alone. Caught in his gaze, I couldn't look away. I wanted to avoid this so very, very much. But I couldn't.

He reached over and caught one of my hands in his. "Jesus, Mae, you're freezing," he said, reaching for my other hand.

His palms were warm and dry as they curled around mine, and his touch was a balm to my unsettled and raw emotions.

"I'm sorry," he repeated.

"You really don't have to apologize," I said through the lump in my throat.

"But I do. I knew something was really wrong, but I didn't know what. I should've known."

"It's okay," I whispered.

"Just to be super clear, you know nothing happened with your roommate, right?"

I nodded quickly. "I did. Everyone filled me in, and she was pissed about it."

"That's kind of beside the point, though, isn't it?" he asked, his tone low and laced with an intensity that surprised me.

"I don't know what you mean."

"Well, my fucking roommate raped you," he said flatly.

"It wasn't your fault," I whispered hoarsely.

"How do we start over?"

Ah, now that was the gigantic question. Encountering a big, bad wolf literally seemed like child's play compared to figuring out how to vanquish my own fears and the memories I'd tried so very hard to bury.

I told myself I should pull my hands away from his, but his touch felt so good. It was such a subtle thing. There was a reason I'd crushed on him before and halfway fallen in love with him. He'd been such a solid, good guy—always strong and stable, always easy and comfortable to be around. I trusted him on a deep level.

As I looked over at him, I thought about the therapist I'd gone to see a few years ago. She'd been really helpful. Thanks to her, I didn't have nightmares anymore even though I'd still hated how things ended for Rowan and me back then. My therapist had told me that trying to date someone might be a crucial step for me. But I didn't hate myself anymore for what happened, and getting to that point had been an internal battle I'd won. I knew I had done the only thing I could have done at the time. All I could do now was go forward. I wondered about reaching out to that therapist. It had been a while, but she would probably love to know Rowan had found me, and we'd reconnected.

"That was what this dinner date was supposed to be about. We were going to start over, and all the shit that happened wasn't going to be between us," he said quietly.

"If there's one thing I know, it's that you can't change the past. It's all there anyway," I rasped.

"Mae, were you going to try to keep that from me forever?"

I blinked as the tears stung my eyes. Shrugging, I replied, "I guess so. I don't want it to define me."

My hands were warming under his touch. His eyes

searched my face. "It doesn't define you, not to me. I hate that it happened, but I'm glad I know."

The emotional fracture created by cutting Rowan out of my life was cracking open slowly. Instead of unbearable pain, it ached, but it also felt as if sunlight was slipping through. What lay behind it was dark and cold, and I was weary of carrying this alone. I had told those few friends in college what happened but then had rarely spoken of it again except in therapy. My college friends had all been decent enough to let me keep it quiet. I simply hadn't been ready for more. I didn't think I could've kept it a secret forever. Yet silence about events gives so much power to secrets. The longer the silence holds, the more powerful the secret becomes.

I took a breath, my chest loosening a little. Rowan's thumb brushed across the back of my hand, the subtle touch soothing me.

"It's weird, but I guess I'm relieved someone else told you."

"I don't think Stephanie would've said anything if I hadn't asked Darryl."

"It's okay. I haven't been in touch with her for years. I know she didn't do it in a gossipy way."

The server arrived with our drinks. I felt a little bereft when Rowan let go of one of my hands to lift his beer. Tendrils of warmth encircled my heart when he kept one hand firmly in mine and laced his fingers through mine. His thumb kept brushing in light strokes, and warmth radiated from his touch, sliding through me like a soft summer breeze in the trees.

I took a swallow of my wine. "Oh, that's good."

"You look surprised," he said with an arch of a brow.

God help me. Even when he lifted a brow, my belly

swooped. "Well, I've never had gooseberry wine. It was kind of a risk."

His eyes crinkled at the corners with his warm smile. He took a swallow from his draft beer, lowering it and commenting, "This is good too."

"There are some good breweries in Alaska. The menu says everything here is from a brewery in Anchorage."

He dipped his head in agreement. "Are we officially changing the subject?"

I needed another sip of my yummy wine. Swallowing, I shrugged. "See, that's why I hate it, why I never wanted you to know. It becomes this thing that sucks up all the air."

"Mae, you were one of my best friends in college, and I thought we had a shot at something more. And then, that was it. You weren't my friend, and I didn't know what happened."

Chapter Nineteen

ROWAN

"I understand why you never wanted me to know, but I could have been there for you. I would've kicked his ass." Just thinking about it sent a bolt of icy anger through me, but now wasn't the time to focus on that emotion.

Mae pressed her lips in a line. "I didn't want anyone to kick his ass. I just wanted to forget about it."

"You could probably still press charges."

I'd spent most of my nights, and every moment when I wasn't occupied, thinking of all the things I wished to befall Chet. I knew I could find him, but I hadn't tried yet. Aside from being there for Mae, I owed her the chance to call the shots on this.

What I really wanted was to find him and cause him more pain than he'd caused Mae, or something along those lines. I didn't trust myself if I got my hands on him, that was for sure.

Mae was really quiet before she shook her head, just barely. "I don't want to."

I opened my mouth to argue the point, but she lifted her palm, so I shut up.

"I know you probably want to kick his ass, or at least see him deal with some legal fallout. I did look into it, and it's not easy. I was pretty out of it and I barely remember anything. It's nothing more than flashes of memories. The reason I know something happened is because it was my first time, and the pain snapped me out of the haze."

Mae spoke so calmly it was as if she was reciting a recipe. My chest and brain felt as if they'd been lit on fire with rage. I clenched my beer glass with my hand and willed myself to stay calm. Mae didn't need to see me lose my shit.

"Are you fucking kidding me?" I finally asked after I took a long swallow of my beer.

She shook her head. "No, look, those date rape drugs are pretty common. You know that, right?"

"What? What do you mean?"

Mae let out a sharp sigh. "There's a nail polish for women to use that changes color if they dip their fingers in a drink and it's been spiked. I'm not alone. I'm just another statistic."

I took another swallow of beer. Fuck.

"I know you want me to do something about it, but my memory's spotty at best. I knew Chet was an asshole."

"That's an understatement."

"I knew you said he was a jerk, but I didn't realize I shouldn't even take a drink from him."

I was so torn up over this that I was reeling. I was not going to fall apart in front of her.

"You have to let me deal with this the way I want to," she continued. "I don't want to press charges, and

I don't want you to find him, and I don't want you to kick his ass."

"What do you want?"

"The chances of it going anywhere legally are close to zero. I did do one thing, and it's the only thing that's given me a little bit of peace."

"What's that?"

"It was a year after it happened, my senior year when we were graduating. I filed a report and warned the school about him. I heard about it happening to another girl, and I didn't want it to happen to anybody else."

"Seriously? I don't know what happened with him after he moved out. Did he graduate?"

She shook her head. "Not from UNC. I know I wasn't the only one who reported him, and he didn't return for what would've been his last semester."

"It doesn't seem like enough," I protested.

Mae shrugged. "That's the world we live in." Her tone was disconcertingly calm while I wanted to punch the universe.

I had enough sense to know reacting with violence was definitely not the solution for the moment. "You don't think he should be charged?" I couldn't help but press once more.

"Rowan, I looked into it. My case is not a good case. There were no witnesses. Just me and my spiked drink."

I felt sick, and my heart ached on a visceral level.

Mae was *that* girl. I'd been so in love with her before. I'd been afraid to ruin our friendship, and I'd wanted to get it right when we finally started dating. I didn't want to be a dumbass like so many guys were back then.

"So, tell me, how do we start over?"

"Now that this giant elephant is in the room between us?" she countered.

"I don't think it's an elephant anymore, but it was before I knew."

She looked at me, her gaze skeptical. "What do you mean?"

"Because it was a secret, a big secret. You didn't have to tell me. Obviously, that was your call. But it's the whole reason we broke up or never really got off the ground. I lost one of my favorite people. You hear those stories about people who lost touch with someone. Every time I heard something like that, I thought about you. I would think about texting you again, figuring you probably had the same number. I never deleted it. But you told me to leave you alone, and I wanted to respect that. I knew you got your graduate degree, but you kept a pretty low profile." Mae's lips twisted in one of her lopsided smiles. Even though my heart was throbbing, a little bit of joy was starting to push through the heavy weight of pain.

"So, we start where we were back then," she chimed in, surprising me.

"How many dates did we go on?" I asked.

"Three," she whispered.

"That's right. Fourth time's the charm."

"Really?" A slow smile unfurled across her face.

"Yeah, and we're gonna get it right this time."

Her gaze sobered, and she took a quick swallow of wine. "Rowan, I don't know. I don't really date."

"Do you trust me?"

She nodded slowly. "You know I do."

"Okay then. We can do this."

Her eyes held mine through several resounding beats of my heart before she nodded.

Chapter Twenty

MAE

It was kind of miraculous, but I actually enjoyed dinner. It was really good to spend time with Rowan again without that giant secret between us. I appreciated that he understood it was my story to tell him, and I could've kept the secret if I chose. I knew it would have gotten in the way for us in the long run, though.

That was the very reason I shut him out back then. Of course, that version of me had been younger and a little less bitter. After what happened, I hadn't known what to do other than batten down the hatches, literally and figuratively.

Rowan insisted on staying a full hour after he finished his beer because he was driving us home. When we got to my house and he walked me to the door, I was pretty sure he was going to leave without kissing me.

"Oh no you don't!" I reached for his hand as he started to step back.

He tried to play it off. "What?"

"You're not leaving. Not without kissing me," I declared.

He stared down at me in the darkness. It was cold enough out that I shivered.

"Inside," he ordered, pointing at the door behind me.

I quickly fished my keys out, and we walked in. After greeting Sassafras, I turned and looked at him. "We already kissed. Why are you not kissing me good night?"

For the first time tonight, Rowan looked a little lost. "Mae—" he began before stopping abruptly.

"No, no, no, no!"

"No, what?"

"Don't let this be an excuse to pretend you can't touch me. We had a really good kiss in the parking lot, and then the other night in the kitchen." I flapped a hand in the direction of the kitchen.

He shifted on his feet uncomfortably. "But—"

Great, just freaking great. He couldn't manage more than a single word without sputtering. "But, what?"

"What?"

"Oh, my god. You know I'm not some innocent virgin."

"Mae! Don't talk about it like that." His eyes were kind of wild.

"Rowan, don't."

This was firing me up in a weird way. I wanted to scream, and I wanted to cry. But more than any of those things, I wanted to kiss him. So I did.

I grabbed his jacket and yanked him to me as I stepped closer. His back thumped against the door when I leaned up and pressed my lips to his. It started out kind of messy because my aim was off, and my mouth landed on the corner of his lips.

Leaning back, I murmured, "See, it's fine."

Rowan held still, his eyes searching mine. The air fairly crackled with tension, and then we were kissing again.

He didn't treat me like I was fragile, but unfortunately, he did put a stop to it. At which point, I was seriously hot and bothered. "Are you really going to go home?" I protested between gasps.

"Yes," he said with a sigh.

I could feel the hot press of his arousal against my hip. "Rowan, come on."

He looked pained. "This is our first date, since our last three dates. I don't want to take advantage."

"I want you to take advantage. I want this," I demanded.

He stared at me. I could hear the clock ticking loudly in the background.

"Mae, I—"

"Rowan, I'm asking you to stay. If I have to strip you naked myself, I will."

As if to emphasize the point, Sassafras hissed in the background from the couch. Rowan's eyes widened. "She's kind of cranky. I think she was mostly napping the last time you were here," I explained.

After another stare down between us, he pushed away from the door and shrugged out of his jacket. I unzipped my jacket, taking them both and hanging them on the hooks by the door. We took off our boots.

"I even wore dressy boots," I offered.

His eyes bounced down and back up to mine. "I noticed. They're hot." He smiled, a sly glint in his eyes.

"Really?"

"Everything about you is hot, Mae. I had such a crush on you back then. You were that girl for me."

"Well, that's good because you were that guy. You still are," I replied, surprising myself with my honesty.

"Why were you so mad when you saw me here at first?" he asked, his gaze sobering.

"I don't know. It just all got tangled up. Seeing you meant I had to deal with why I stopped being friends with you."

"I felt like you sliced me out of your life with a surgical knife."

Since I was already being honest, I didn't stop. "That's pretty much what I did. You were still room-mates with him, and I didn't know what to do."

"Only for like another month, and then it was the end of the semester." He shook his head. "I'm sorry. I get it. I do. I'm just relieved it wasn't something I did even though I kind of wish it had been."

"Never," I whispered.

I was getting lost in the brilliant green of his eyes, and he kissed me again. One kiss blurred into the next and then the next. I didn't know how long we stood there in the living room kissing until he lifted his head and said, "Bedroom."

Chapter Twenty-One

ROWAN

My hands were practically shaking. This was not what I expected tonight.

I told myself I wasn't going to let it go this far, yet I was caught in the midst of competing impulses. I wanted Mae. I wanted this. With a truly, madly, deeply kind of want.

And, sweet Jesus, I had wanted Mae for what felt like forever at this point. Seriously. I crushed on her so hard in college, and then I'd finally asked her out. A few kisses later, and it all ended so abruptly.

Here she was now, more beautiful than she was back then. I didn't even know how that was possible. She'd filled out some, and she didn't look so young anymore. I was afraid I was going to mess this up.

Someone had raped her, and I didn't know how to make it right. Despite my thoughts hammering away, she wasn't letting me dwell.

She was peeling off her jeans. My mouth had gone dry, and my cock was as hard as a baseball bat.

"Wait!"

Mae stopped with her hands curled over the waistband of her jeans. Turning to face me, she hitched her brows up in question. In three strides, I was standing right in front of her. Lifting a hand, I brushed her hair away from her face. Her lips were pink and kiss-bitten.

"I don't want to rush," I murmured.

Her eyes searched mine, and I could hear the thud of my heartbeat echoing through my body. Everything was coiled tight inside, and I craved a release. Yet I had to say what came next. I couldn't *not* say it.

"We don't have to do this tonight."

Vulnerability flickered in her eyes, disappearing so fast I wouldn't have recognized it if I didn't know her so well. Every time I thought about what had actually happened now that I knew the truth, it felt as if a knife was being twisted in my heart, again and again and again. I also wanted to break Chet into pieces. I wasn't a violent guy, but holy hell.

He'd known Mae was my friend, and I hated thinking this, but that's probably part of why he went after her. He was always about just taking whatever he wanted.

"I know we don't have to," she said, her husky voice bringing me back to this moment. "But I want to."

I took in a gulp of air. "Okay, but we can stop at any point. I don't care when. All you have to do is say so."

"I know," she whispered. "But that is exactly why I won't want to stop."

"What do you mean?"

"Because I know you will if I ask."

My heart ached as I nodded. "I don't have a condom." I heard myself blurting out.

After learning Mae's truth, I had told myself I

wouldn't have expectations, so I had consciously left any protection at home.

She stared at me quietly. "I have an IUD." She paused, and she caught her bottom lip with her teeth, worrying it. "After what happened, I've always been really careful."

"Mae." Her name came out in a ragged and raw whisper.

"Stop. Just stop feeling bad. You can't change the past. Trust me, I wish I could," she said, her chin lifting and her eyes glittering with determination. "Please, please don't let that screw everything up. I missed you. I know it's my own fault we stopped talking."

I shook my head sharply, sliding my hand down to palm the side of her neck. "It's not your fault. Even though I didn't understand then, I understand now. It was easier to be mad, and you probably needed to be mad."

The sound of her swallowing was audible. "I did."

"I've never had sex without a condom."

"Really?" Her eyes widened at this.

I shrugged. "Uh, yeah. My dad lectured me about it repeatedly. My point being, I know I'm clean."

We stood there, and uncertainty started to slide through me. Not because I didn't want this. Holy fucking hell, I wanted this. I wanted Mae, and I trusted that she thought she wanted this, but it still had to be her call.

She uncurled one of her hands from over her waistband, placing it on the center of my chest. My heart lunged toward the heat of her touch as she leaned up and brushed her lips over mine, making an indecipherable sound in her throat. Once again, the moment I was kissing Mae I forgot everything else. Her mouth was divine, and she tasted a little sweet.

I was careful not to let my need and fierce lust take over by being gentle and not getting rough with her clothes. Jesus, I wanted to yank everything off. I forced myself to let her take the lead. It wasn't as if that was a hardship. Her questing hands mapped my chest and impatiently yanked at my shirt until I reached behind my head and tugged it off in one swoop somewhere along the way. She'd ditched her blouse and bra, and her skin felt so good. The tight points of her nipples pressed into my skin.

At one point, she got impatient. "Rowan!" She pushed at my shoulder, and I reluctantly lifted my head from where I'd been making love to a sweet spot right behind her ear.

She had goose bumps rising on her skin, and her cheeks were flushed pink.

"What?" I asked.

"Stop being so careful," she ordered.

"I'm not being careful." That was sort of a lie.

"Yes, you are. You're waiting for me to make every single first move. That's ridiculous. I want you, and you want me." At this, she boldly stroked her hand over my aching arousal tucked behind my jeans. Another shot of blood arrowed down.

I shook my head to try to think. "What are you asking?"

"Stop thinking. Stop worrying. You didn't the other night in the kitchen."

"Oh no, I definitely did not," I replied with a husky chuckle.

"I promise I'll say something if it's not okay."

It felt as if the reins of control were sliding through my fingers because then she pushed me back and finally shimmied out of her jeans. She had on this silky scrap of underwear.

That was it. The reins slid through my fingers, and a whip cracked through the air, lightning sizzling around us. In a fiery second, her deft fingers unsnapped the button on my jeans and slid the zipper down. I kicked my jeans free, and then we were on the bed.

She was warm and soft everywhere. Sweet sighs, whimpers, and moans surrounded us. I mapped her body, my lips lingering on every curve, teasing her nipples, my hand sliding over her trembling belly. A groan escaped when I discovered the silk between her thighs was damp. I already knew how she felt there, wet silk clenching around my fingers.

"Rowan!" she cried out.

She shimmied, and I tugged her panties down. I charted a path with my lips over the curve of her belly, dallying on the sensitive skin just on the inside of her pelvic bone. I slid my palms up her thighs, pushing her knees apart. Dipping my head, I tasted her. She was tangy and salty, and her hips bucked against my mouth.

She came faster than I expected with a shudder against me and a rough cry. Then she was yanking me closer. I almost froze because this part of it was hard.

Without a word, I shifted up and rolled onto my back. She had plenty of pillows on her bed, and I shimmied back until I was propped against them.

Her hand curled around my cock, and she smeared her thumb over the cum already dripping out. She surprised me when she leaned down and gave me a teasing swirl with her tongue.

"Come here," I murmured.

And she did. Her big ginger eyes were boring into

mine, and I felt my heart kick hard enough to crack a rib. This girl was everything. It had only ever been us. I remember thinking I'd been the luckiest guy when we kissed the first time.

But then, it all got blown to smithereens. Maybe luck was on my side now. We were both older and wiser, smart enough to know when we had a good thing.

I watched as she rose over me, her breasts bouncing. I couldn't resist, leaning forward and catching one of her damp pink nipples with my mouth. I gave it a sharp suck, and her fingers speared my hair when she cried out. My head thumped against the headboard behind me.

I felt the kiss of her slick heat. I held my breath, resisting the urge to thrust into her. She slid down swiftly, closing her eyes and taking a deep breath. When they opened, everything blurred as I lost myself in her gaze and the silky clench of the very heart of her.

Chapter Twenty-Two

MAE

Rowan stared at me. I couldn't look away from the beam of his gaze. My body was a cacophony of sensation. But amidst the intensity of it all, a sense of triumph rose through.

Finally, *finally*. I had erased an ugly experience with this one.

Not for a second did I think of what had happened before. All I knew at this moment was Rowan and the feel of him filling me. Bonus point: firefighters are pure muscle. He was *all* of that. His hands slid down to my hips, gripping just enough to let me know he was there.

I was impatient and rose again, demanding, "Don't be gentle. Fuck me."

His grip tightened, and he rocked into me deeply. My eyes fell closed as I took a shuddering breath. I didn't expect what came next. He'd already given me one orgasm with his mouth and his fingers, and I thought that was enough. After several deep strokes, he held me closer and rocked into me in subtle nudges.

My breasts brushed against his chest when he whispered, "Mae, I need to see you."

I dragged my eyes open. It felt as if intimacy was binding us in a shimmering net, like glittery sparks flying from a bonfire encircling us. His green eyes were hot on mine. His thumbs pressed right over my clit. My orgasm startled me, the force of it so intense I cried out keenly. My mind blanked, and I swear I saw stars.

I felt him shudder with one deep surge into me, followed with the heat of his release filling me. His arms wrapped around me, and I fell against him, tucking my head into the curve of his neck as we trembled together. I didn't know how long he held me like that, but my awareness returned in pieces. The sensations ricocheting through me slowed. His fingers sifted through my hair. I felt the press of his hand still gripping my hip, his collarbone under my lips, and the feel of his heartbeat slowing in tune with mine. I didn't want this to end because it was so much better than I thought. I did trust him completely, and I'd already known that. Even then, I'd worried. But this experience was so separate from what had happened before. The fragmented memories didn't bombard me as I'd feared they might.

I eventually lifted my head to find his gaze waiting. We stared at each other quietly for a moment, and I felt my lips tug into a lopsided smile.

He leaned forward and kissed me. His gaze was almost bemused.

"What?" I pressed.

He lifted his shoulder lightly in a shrug. "I don't know. That just felt really good. Better than really good. Better than amazing."

I rolled my eyes. "Better than amazing?"

After the intensity of that and all the emotion attached to it, I needed the lightness. When he laughed, I could feel the reverberation of it in my body. Because he was that kind of man, he lifted me off his lap and carted me into the shower. We fell asleep together.

I came awake to the feel of Rowan shifting behind me into a shivering stretch. I felt every vibration of his body down to my toes. He was a toe-curling kind of guy. He was spooned behind me, and I lay there blinking as a smile curled the corners of my mouth.

I almost laughed, and then realized I actually had when he asked, "What's so funny?"

I felt the rumble of his voice between my shoulder blades. "Nothing really." I rolled over on my back, feeling a little sheepish. "I never thought I'd wake up with you."

His eyes skated over my face when his lips stretched into a smile, and my belly did a little shimmy and twist. We stared at each other, and it felt kind of silly. He lifted a hand, smoothing my tangled hair.

"It's really pretty awesome," he murmured before dusting a kiss over my lips.

That glancing touch sent a sizzle zipping through my body. He rose, resting on an elbow as the sheets slid down to his waist. I sighed and elbowed him in the side.

"What?"

"You're kind of too much."

"Too much what?"

I waved vaguely at his chest. "All manly and muscley," I offered by way of explanation.

He chuckled. "My job's kind of demanding."

"True. You actually have to stay in shape."

"What are your plans for today?" he prompted.

I straightened, feeling a little bashful and tugging the sheet with me. I saw Rowan's eyes, or rather felt Rowan's eyes, dip down to my nipples, which were telling him good morning by perking up. My cheeks got hot, and he was gracious enough to let me keep the sheet tucked under my armpits.

Sassafras jumped on the bed, coming to a quick stop as her tail twitched in the air. She appeared to be attempting to assess the situation.

"Does she normally sleep with you?" Rowan asked.

"Um, no, not really. Sometimes she does, and sometimes she doesn't, but I don't think she's ever stayed in bed all night, that's for sure."

"I don't think she likes me."

Sassafras sank her haunches on the bed, her tail slithering back and forth like a snake on the sheets. "Aunt Carrie said she needed me."

"I think she probably figured her cats were more than enough," Rowan offered, his tone dry.

"You know her cats?" I prompted.

The rumble of his chuckle reverberated through me. "Carrie's a regular with the fire department. Her older cat is known to get stuck in trees. It's a rite of passage to go rescue him. I've already had to do it twice because she's got a kitten now too."

I sputtered a laugh. "Of course, she does. I didn't know her older cat got stuck in trees that often, though."

"Your plans?" he asked.

"I don't have any plans. Would you like some pancakes for breakfast?"

Chapter Twenty-Three

ROWAN

Mae made us pancakes for breakfast. They were light and fluffy, and she sprinkled chocolate chips on them. The fact that she remembered I loved chocolate chip pancakes was more sweet than bitter. But there was definitely a tinge of bitter because I'd missed seven years with her.

Obviously, I couldn't predict how things would've turned out, but I was pretty sure we would have stayed together. I loved her already. I just didn't know if she was ready for me to unload that on her.

We went from pancakes to her insisting that we should go for a walk even though it was snowing. Snow was floating from the sky in plump flakes, and she wanted me to see her favorite waterfall.

The day was beyond good. I hiked with her to see a small waterfall that poured over a cliff in the forest. It was definitely worth the twenty-minute hike into the frosty trees. After the hike, we decided to swing by Firehouse Café for hot chocolate. Mae promised me she would spike the hot chocolate when we got back to her place.

Janet was smiling at us when we reached the counter. "You two seem like you've known each other for a long time," she commented.

Mae's cheeks were tinged pink as she nodded and dipped her chin. "We were in college together."

Janet's sharp gaze bounced back and forth between Mae and me before her smile flashed again. "Well, what can I get you?"

"Mae says I need to try your peppermint hot chocolate," I replied.

"We need it to go because I'm spiking it," Mae chimed in.

Janet's laughter rang out. "That's the way to do it. You know, I can serve alcohol after six."

Mae glanced at her watch. It was five thirty. Just then, the bell over the door announced someone's arrival. Mae glanced back, and her flush deepened.

"Well, you're about to meet her parents. I hope you're ready," Janet said, sotto voce.

Mae cast a faux glare at Janet, and Janet simply grinned. "I'll get those hot chocolates. Peppermint for both of you?"

At Mae's nod, Janet turned and began prepping our drinks.

"Hi, sweetie," the woman I presumed was Mae's mother said as she stopped at her side and gave her a quick hug.

Although Mae's mother's hair had faded from a honey blond to a more silvery shade, they shared similar coloring. Mae's father cast me an alert look, but he waited patiently before stepping to Mae's side and dropping a quick kiss on her cheek.

"This is Rowan," Mae said, gesturing to me. "This is my mother, Barbara, and this is my father, Daniel."

I shook both of their hands. "Nice to meet you both."

Mae's mother appeared almost bursting with excitement. I wasn't sure what she was going to do, and then suddenly, she hugged me. "It is *so* nice to meet you."

Mae let out a soft sigh. "Mom, please don't make this weird," she pleaded.

Barbara waved her off. "This is your friend from college, right? You used to talk about Rowan all the time. You said you were going to bring him to Alaska, and then you never did."

I could practically feel the tension vibrating from Mae. Her eyes narrowed, and my gut clenched. She had the look she'd had the whole last month of that fated semester and the following year when I hardly ever saw her. Her features were stiff—very careful, very controlled. I knew without her telling me that she'd never told her parents what happened. Although my heart was already broken and cracked wide open over what happened to her, this somehow made it hurt even more. I hated that she handled it alone.

"Well, he's here now," Mae said brightly.

Janet handed me the hot chocolates. I had already put cash on the counter, and she snatched it up while Mae wasn't paying attention. "I'm a hotshot firefighter," I explained when Mae's mother asked me what I did.

Her father nodded as if he approved. "Plenty of those around here."

"Very true." With Willow Brook the base for three crews, the area had more than enough firefighters. Alaska needed firefighters because it was a big state, and much of the land had a high fire risk.

Mae's parents hadn't even looked toward Janet until Mae finally said, "Mom, it's your turn."

"Oh!" Barbara squeaked while her father chuckled.

"Would you like to come to dinner?" her mother asked next as her father stepped to the counter.

"Mom," Mae ground out, her tone laced with warning.

"I'd love to have dinner sometime if it's all right with Mae."

When Mae looked at me, I could see the gratitude in her eyes as she mouthed, "Thank you," over her shoulder.

"You just make your plans with Mae, and I'll be there," I offered. "I'll make sure she knows my schedule."

"Excellent, excellent." Her mother clasped her hands together in front of her chest, squeezing them together tightly.

"It was great to see you. We're going to go, Mom," Mae piped up.

Her dad caught my eyes. "Good to meet you."

"Yes, great to meet you both," I replied.

After that, Mae practically dragged me out. "I'm so sorry," she said hurriedly once we were outside. "My mom is enthusiastic, and she really wants me to date."

An icy gust of wind blew Mae's hair into a swirl. I slipped my hand through her elbow, and we hurried to my SUV. I'd left it running while we were in the café, so it was plenty warm. "It was nice to meet your parents, and you don't need to apologize," I said once we were inside.

"I know, but they kind of put you on the spot, so I'm sorry about that."

I reached over and snagged her hand in mine.

"Hey, that's okay. I'd love to have dinner with you and your parents."

She eyed me dubiously.

"You don't get it, do you?"

"Get what?" she asked.

"I was pretty devastated when you stopped talking to me. I get it now. I totally get it. But I missed you. You were one of my best friends, and I thought it might be a lot more. Then it wasn't. So being here in Alaska and finally reconnecting with you? Well, I want to do everything with you. I want to meet your parents. I want to have dinner. I want to go grocery shopping. I want to hear you come home from work and be tired. I want to argue about who's going to clean the toilet. I want to persuade your cranky cat, who doesn't seem to like either one of us, to love me."

Mae stared at me, and her mouth dropped open. She started blinking rapidly just before tears spilled down her cheeks.

"Hey, hey, I didn't mean to make you cry." I leaned across the console, wrapping an arm around her. "Don't cry. Or maybe cry. Whatever. I don't want to tell you what to feel."

I was a little dismayed because I didn't know what to do with a crying Mae. "I'm sorry I didn't tell you what happened," she murmured into my chest.

My heart gave an achy thump. "You didn't have to tell me then or now."

She lifted her head, and I nudged her chin up with my knuckles. "Yeah, but it sucks. I hate, I fucking hate, what happened."

"I do too. If I could trade it and have it be something I did, I would, by the way. But I get it. Let's just focus on right now. We can't change the past."

She nodded jerkily, and I brushed her tears away

with my thumb. I reached into my glove compartment, hoping there would be tissues there. "Fuck, I don't have any tissues," I muttered.

Mae giggled between sniffles. "You're not a tissue guy, Rowan. I have some in my purse."

She reached down and snagged her purse off the floor, tugging some tissues out and blowing her nose.

"I need to say something."

Her eyes whipped up to mine.

I managed to speak over the rush of blood in my ears with every beat of my heart. "I love you. I was in love with you then, but I didn't understand it until it was too late."

Her palm flew to her chest, and she took several shuddering breaths. "I loved you too, and I still do. I don't think I ever stopped." She let out a deep sigh before her forehead fell to the curve of my neck. "We lost a lot of time." I felt the motion of her lips on my collarbone.

"We can't change the past, Mae. Maybe this time, we'll get it right. We were pretty young back then. We could have totally fucked it up."

She lifted her head. "I don't think so. We were really close."

My heart was still drumming fast, and joy was rushing with every beat. "I know. That's why I was afraid to tell you I totally had it bad for you." She smiled. "I had it so bad for you. Still do, by the way, even when the timing isn't right."

"What do you mean? We got the timing right this time."

"I mean, this is kind of a heavy conversation, and my body isn't getting the memo." I placed her hand over my swollen and aching arousal.

Her eyes went wide. "Oh," she breathed. "Well,

we'd better hurry home. Hurry." She elbowed me in the side.

"Don't worry, it's not going anywhere. We're going back to your house, and you're going to spike this hot chocolate because I want to enjoy that first."

Mae cast me a sly grin, her palm stroking over my arousal. "We can always reheat it."

———

I meant what I said back when we were leaving Firehouse Café, but Mae had other ideas, and she was persuasive. As soon as we were in her house, her cat eyed both of us for a moment from the back of the living room couch before walking out slowly, tail held high and twitching.

Mae crossed to the kitchen and set our hot chocolates on the counter after she kicked off her boots and hung up her jacket. I was following her to the kitchen when she met me halfway and pressed her palm on my chest.

"I meant what I said."

"What?" I countered, a little slow to catch up.

She dragged her palm over my still hard cock. Because she was Mae, and I was me, and it was near impossible to turn the dial down on my lust. It had been bottled up for too long. Not to say that I'd been chaste, but I hadn't been serious with anyone. Every time I considered something other than casual, Mae was always in the back of my mind while I wondered what had happened with us.

She was the spark. Just her. I sucked my breath in when she bit her lip and looked up at me. Her cheeks were flushed pink from the cold.

"I meant what I said too," I protested, trying to rally my discipline. It was a weak argument.

Mae grinned. "Your mouth says one thing, but your body says another."

In a hot second, she was unbuttoning my jeans. Her cool palm slid into my boxers, the shock of her touch making my cock leap under it.

"Fuck, Mae," I gasped.

She giggled, murmuring, "Here, let me warm you up."

Her warm mouth closed over the tip of my cock, and her tongue swirled around it while she shoved my jeans down around my hips. Then there she was, kneeling in front of me and angling her head to glance up. The sly, dark gleam in her eyes sent desire zipping through me hot and fast. It was always there on low simmer around her. She turned the flame up on high and poured gasoline on it.

She said something—hell if I knew what—and I felt the vibration of it around my cock when she took me in her mouth. This time when her palm gripped me, it was warm, and she teased me until my control was frayed. I tried to regain it, but she was having none of it.

"Come on, Rowan," she whispered.

"Mae!" I choked out.

She paused and leaned back, releasing my cock with a little pop. "Just give me this," she said, seeming to enjoy having me at her mercy.

It wasn't like I could refuse anything Mae wanted. So, when she dragged her tongue slowly along the underside of my cock before taking me in her mouth again, my release came in a rush. As I clung to her hair, she drank me down. I was still trembling from the force of my climax when she sat back on her heels, looking up with a satisfied grin.

I tugged her to her feet, and we stumbled across the room, one kiss blurring into the next. I meant to take it slow, but that was a major challenge with her. It didn't take much for me to be ready all over again.

Before I knew it, I was sliding her jeans down over her hips, and her round bottom was tempting me with a glimpse of pink glistening at the apex of her thighs. I teased my fingers there, finding her slick and hot.

"Fuck, Mae," I choked out.

"Well, you could just do that." She glanced over her shoulder.

This version of Mae with her guard down, teasing and saucy, was so much more than I expected. My heart kicked hard in my chest. I leaned over, pressing a kiss to that sweet spot just below her ear, savoring how she shivered and let out a little whimper when I sank two fingers inside her.

Chapter Twenty-Four

MAE

This Rowan was a man I hadn't known before. Being with him like this, having him at my mercy moments ago gave me a sense of power I hadn't known I even wanted.

For all these years, I'd worried I'd never be able to relax. But with Rowan, I felt completely safe. Maybe time had passed, and maybe we'd lost something. In a way, though, we'd gained so much more. I knew him, and he was true and solid.

One of his palms slid over my bottom, giving me a squeeze. The calloused surface sent sparks scattering over my skin and goose bumps prickling everywhere. I felt fluid, melting like honey in the sun under his touch.

We were still half-dressed. We'd gotten my shirt off, but my bra was on, hanging loose, and he still had his shirt on. He said something—I didn't even know what—before he growled my name in that sexy voice. I wanted him inside me. *Now.*

"Rowan, hurry," I ordered, arching and pressing back into his touch.

His fingers disappeared from teasing me, and I felt the thick press of his cock at my entrance. He held still, and I arched back again, letting out a low moan at the thick slide as he filled me and seated himself deeply.

I was already teetering on the edge of my release, spun so tight inside I felt reckless and restless, and I needed everything to spin loose. I sensed he was still trying to be gentle, but that's not what I wanted. I met his thrusts roughly, and he followed my lead with one hand gripping my hip tightly. I loved the feel of it, how his fingers pressed into the give of my skin. Then he drew back, sinking in slowly a few times until my own restless motion kicked up the pace, and he was pounding into me, saying, "Mae, tell me if it's too much."

"It's not. Stop worrying," I gasped.

I never thought I'd be the one telling someone to stop worrying, but that was the gift Rowan gave me. I could forget myself. I could let go with him. I felt it the second he stopped worrying. His motions became rougher, his grip tighter on my hip, and his voice hoarser.

With every sound, every motion, every sensation, my need coiled tighter and tighter until he murmured something. One hand slid around my waist, and his fingers were magic. He knew just how to touch me, not that it took much. I felt like a bomb about to go off, and the second he exerted the slightest pressure over my slippery and swollen clit, I detonated. Pleasure exploded as I shuddered roughly and cried out. He followed me over the edge only seconds later.

I loved that I could feel his release filling me. "Mae!" he gasped in a ragged shout.

My hands were gripping the back of the couch

tightly with one of my knees pressing into the cushions. I was shaking all over from the force of my release. He curled around me, his grip loosening on my hip and his touch turning soothing as his hand smoothed up my spine. I felt hot kisses dropping in a crooked line down to my waist. The intimacy of this moment was intense and almost overwhelming.

While the other night we'd been facing each other, something about this felt deeper. I'd let my control go and handed it to him. He trusted that I wanted him to have it. My heart felt raw and exposed, and all of this was happening so very fast.

A few moments later, we disentangled. When I turned and met his eyes for a flash, I felt bashful and so exposed it almost hurt. But I saw the same thing in his eyes, and it was okay. Because this was Rowan, and he was my friend first. And I knew him.

There were those friends that you had—usually not very many—when it was just easy, right from the very beginning. That was what I had with Rowan. Now, we had all of this. It felt like a glittering gift handed to me. I felt as if a curtain had been pulled back on a universe I hadn't even known existed, but it was fragile to the touch.

He helped me pull my clothes back together. I pulled his zipper up and buttoned his jeans. After that, I spiked our hot chocolate with vanilla vodka, and we watched *Schitt's Creek* together. He stayed over again, and I discovered I wasn't even that worried about him having dinner with my parents. It would be fine. They could finally be happy that I was dating someone. We'd almost skipped past that with Rowan telling me he loved me and me owning my own feelings.

Chapter Twenty-Five

ROWAN

Thanksgiving was less than a week away, and I was feeling torn because I didn't want to leave right now. Not with Mae and I feeling so good. But I had two more phone calls from my parents and another one from my sister, who was super pissed off at them. I knew I needed to go to Stolen Hearts Valley.

I was at Mae's house every night. I was helping her tear out that shag carpet, and we were going to redo the whole interior. I only wanted to spend time with Mae, so it was perfect. One night we were watching TV, and I told her, "I don't want to go to my parents' for Thanksgiving."

She looked over. "To North Carolina?"

I nodded quickly. "It's either that or Christmas, and my sister's having some problems."

"Oh, no. What's wrong?" Her brow creased with worry.

"I think she's dating an asshole, and he sounds controlling. My parents are stressing big time. I'd like to see if I can help."

In the back of my thoughts was the chance to do a little reconnaissance and see if I could track down Chet. I had resisted the urge to do anything about it yet because I knew Mae might not want me to. It was killing me to just let him get away with fucking raping her.

"Well, then you should go," she said firmly.

"I don't want to leave you," I said honestly.

Her smile was warm. "I don't want you to go, but I'm not the kind of girlfriend who needs you with me all the time. I *am* the kind of girlfriend who thinks family matters. I know your family's important to you, so you should go. We'll have Christmas together."

Not that I needed more reasons, but this was why Mae was so perfect. "All right, I'll go. I'm probably going to call you two or three times a day."

"Okay, you can. We can cook our own Thanksgiving dinner when you get back."

———

Mae took me to the airport, giving me a kiss before I went through security.

She peered up at me. "I'll see you when you get back."

Fuck, I didn't want to leave. I held her, maybe too long, lingering until my flight was called the second time. "You have to go," she said with a laugh as she pushed me away.

As soon as I got to North Carolina the following morning, I was glad I was there. I missed Mae like crazy, but my sister hadn't come home the night before and wasn't answering her cell phone. My parents were beyond worried.

"All right, tell me who the hell this guy is. You gave me his name, but tell me everything you know," I said to my parents as we sat at the kitchen table.

My mother's eyes were red and puffy while my father had a stoic but really stressed look on his face.

"Where is she?" I asked, glancing between them.

My mother shook her head slowly. "We don't know."

"Okay, where does he live?" I looked toward my father for this one because he had friends on the local police force.

"His parents are new to the area. I do know where they live. I've spoken to the police."

"I'm going to go over there," I said once my father recited the address so I could put it in my maps.

"Her boyfriend's eighteen," my mother interjected.

"So what? That just means more consequences for him."

I stood, and my father followed me out to the front room. "Son," he began.

"You don't need to worry, Dad. I'll find Colbie. She'll be home for Thanksgiving, and we're gonna figure out what the fuck is going on with this guy," I said flatly.

"You know the drill, but be careful. The police have been called more than once to help de-escalate these assholes. His parents get into it plenty."

I ignored the bolt of anger.

"I'm just having a hard time believing your sister ended up with a guy like this," he added.

"Dad, you know it never starts that way. Assholes like that tend to be charming at first. She's young. I'll be back."

I left, calling my cousin Lucas on the way. He

picked up on the first ring. "Hey, man, are you here for Thanksgiving?"

"Of course."

"I hear we're coming over to your place," Lucas replied with a chuckle.

"That's what I hear. Hey, man, I need to pick your brain for a second."

"What's up?"

"So, my sister's dating a jerk," I began.

"I've heard," Lucas interjected.

"Oh, you have?"

"Yeah, your dad hasn't spoken to me about it, but rumors travel. Stolen Hearts Valley isn't all that big. You know how it goes. EMTs and the police have dealt with him a few times, and his dad's a total ass. Like father like son," my cousin said matter-of-factly.

"Ah, fuck," I muttered.

"You need anything?"

"Well, I want to go talk to him. Mind coming with me?"

"Of course not."

"You on call?" Lucas was a first responder for a mountain crew, so he'd need to stay put if he was.

"Nope. I'm home."

"Can I swing by and pick you up?"

"Absolutely. I'll meet you outside. You can see Valentina and the girls at Thanksgiving."

Minutes later, I pulled up in front of Lucas's place just as he was coming out the front door. He was shrugging into his jacket as he jogged down the steps.

"How's it going?" he asked as soon as he climbed in the car, leaning over to give me a quick side hug.

"Good to see you, but not thrilled with what's going on with my sister," I replied.

"No shit. Fuck, man. I don't even like thinking about Rylie growing up."

"I get it. So, tell me where this guy hangs out."

"I already did a little looking into him while I was waiting for you to show up."

Lucas quickly recited two addresses, starting with his parents'. We rolled by, but there wasn't a single vehicle there.

"Okay, let's head to his apartment. Not that you're worried, but I did notify the police we might be visiting him," Lucas offered.

"You mean I can't just kick this guy's ass?"

"I don't think that would be smart," Lucas replied dryly.

I gritted my teeth. I knew he was right, but still.

A short while later, we pulled up in front of a duplex on a narrow road just off the main highway. A single car was there, which Lucas confirmed belonged to the boyfriend.

We had agreed to go in together. I knew this was going to piss my sister off, but at this point, I wanted this guy to leave her alone. We knocked on the door, and a young guy answered the door. I could see my sister sitting on the couch in the background.

"Hey, sis," I called over the guy's shoulder, ignoring him to begin with.

"Who the fuck are you?" he demanded.

My sister stood at this point. Larry glanced over his shoulder, saying to her, "How the fuck do you know this guy?"

"He's my brother," she said quickly. Colbie slipped past him to give me a hug.

Stepping back, I held her by the shoulders. "You want to go wait in the car?"

Her eyes bounced like a ping pong from me to Lucas to her boyfriend and back to me. "Rowan, I—"

"You're not staying here. I know you're gonna be upset about it, but that's the deal."

"Who the fuck do you think you are? You aren't telling her what to do," Larry interjected.

Dropping my hands from my sister's shoulders, I narrowed my eyes and turned to face him. "Here's the deal. The police are on backup. She's going to the car."

My sister opened her mouth to say something, at which point Larry did me a favor. He didn't even look her way when he ordered, "Get the fuck out and don't come back."

Colbie dashed past him, grabbing her purse and hurrying back out to the car. I could tell she was trying not to cry, but I'd have to deal with that later. Lucas had remained quiet.

"And who the fuck are you?" Larry asked.

"Is that your only question?" I countered sharply.

"She's old enough to decide who she wants to hang out with."

"She's sixteen, and you're eighteen. I don't give a fuck about anything other than you being a controlling asshole. If anything happens, you get big boy charges," I said flatly.

As soon as I heard the car door slam shut outside, I thumped my fingers on his chest, pushing him back through the door. Lucas crowded behind me and kicked the door shut.

"Here's the deal: leave her alone, or I will make your life a living hell. You are not to spend time with her. You are not to hang out with her. You will stop calling her, lose her number, all of it."

Larry narrowed his eyes, sneering a little. "You

know, trying to make her stay away from me is gonna make her want me more."

I wanted to vomit all over the guy's chest. Fisting his shirt in my hand, I pulled his face to mine. "No, it's not. She has better options. We know the scoop on your father, and we know the scoop on what you're doing in the background. Either way, your life is going to be hell. But you keep her tangled up in it, and we'll make it more hell."

"You don't even fucking live here," he sputtered as I let go and shoved him back.

In all honesty, he wasn't putting up much of a fight, which made me even more angry. He was the kind of guy who only bullied people who were smaller than him. He was outnumbered, and he didn't have a chance against Lucas and me.

"I'll stay in town until I make sure you're out of her fucking life."

"Plus," Lucas chimed in. "I'm here all the time, and I'm her cousin. I'm on the first responder crew. We're everywhere all the time. We know your family's history. We know everything. Whether or not Colbie's brother is around, we've got her back."

Larry glared at us. "Whatever. She sucks in bed anyway."

My fist drew back and cracked him on the jaw before I could even think. Lucas simply watched while Larry cried out sharply, cradling his face.

We left. Before we got in the car, Lucas stopped to call the police, giving them an update because he had promised to do so. I was trying to figure out how the fuck my sister ended up with this guy. We climbed in the car, and Colbie was fuming in the back seat.

"What did you do?" she spit out.

"We'll talk in a minute," I said.

"Rowan, I'm going back in."

She started to climb out, and I was profoundly grateful there were childproof locks on this car.

Turning, I eyed her. "If you hang out with him, we will get him arrested. He's dealing meth on the side."

"No, he's not," she protested.

"Yeah, he is," Lucas said flatly, turning to look at her.

"How do you know?" she pressed.

"You know my job. I'm on the first responder crew. We coordinate with the police all the time. Larry deals drugs with his father. It's a family business," Lucas explained.

"Things have been really hard for him," Colbie insisted, although her voice was quieter.

Once we got onto the highway, I pulled off at a rest area so we could finish this conversation before we got home. "You want to know what he said about you?" I asked.

"What?" she muttered, her arms crossing like a guardrail in front of her chest.

"That you suck in bed," I said flatly. "That's what this guy's willing to say about you to your brother and your cousin. He's an asshole." My sister burst into tears, and I pressed on. "He thinks this is going to make you want him more. What you have to understand is this guy doesn't care about you. He's just using you."

"You can't control who I see," she argued.

"I know I can't, but I'm not gonna sit back and let this happen."

"Well, what are you gonna do? Move home?" she muttered as she swiped at her tears with her palms before fishing for a tissue in her purse and blowing her nose.

"If that's what has to happen, I will," I replied sharply.

"You don't need to move home," Lucas interjected. "Now that I know what's going on, I'll keep my ear to the ground. And you know I've got the connections to make sure he's under a fucking microscope. I've already talked to the cops."

My sister swung her tearstained face toward Lucas. "Are you serious?"

He shrugged. "Absolutely. You know who you need to talk to?"

"I don't need to talk to anybody!" Colbie burst out.

Lucas continued, "I'm going to take you out to the lodge. You can have a little chat with my friend Shay."

My sister rolled her eyes. "Why do I want to talk to Shay?"

"Because she knows how things go when you stay with guys like that. Her ex beat her in a fucking parking lot, and that was the only reason he got arrested," Lucas said flatly.

Colbie sagged into the seat. The fight seemed to have gone out of her, and she fell silent for the rest of the drive. After I dropped Lucas off and we returned home, she refused to speak to my parents. She walked straight upstairs into her bedroom and slammed the door.

After filling my parents in, I went to bed. Colbie had my old bedroom, so I was sleeping on a pullout couch in my mother's office. Once I was in bed, I leaned against the pillows and texted Mae.

Me: *Miss you. How are you?*

Her reply came in seconds.

Mae: *Miss you too. I'm fine. What are you doing up so late?*

I decided to call her rather than do this text dance. She answered on the first ring. "Hey."

The second I heard her voice, the tension that had been bundled tight around my chest and shoulders started to loosen.

"Hey..."

I filled her in on the events with my sister. Mae was a good listener, and it was a relief to talk to her. "All you can do is be there for her. It's hard when you're young."

"I know, but fuck. I'm worried this is gonna push her away."

"Maybe. But it sounds like he has the incentive to stay away."

"I hope so."

"Keeping her safe is important, but you're going to have to let her feel her way through not blaming herself for dating an asshole once she can think clearly about it."

"I know." I sighed, leaning my head back. "Tell me what's happening there."

"You've only been gone for two days," she replied, her laughter soft and spinning warmth around my heart. She quickly filled me in on her day at work and her cat's antics. I wanted to stay up all night talking to her.

"Can we watch a show together?"

"What do you mean?"

"You're home, and I have a TV, so we can hang together on the phone and watch something."

"Okay, what are we watching?" I could feel the smile in her voice.

"*Schitt's Creek*. I don't know what episode we're on, though."

"Hang on, I can tell here."

I fell asleep after two episodes. I woke up the next morning to find my sister sulking in the kitchen. She informed me that Larry was refusing to return her texts. I wanted to say thank fucking god, but all I said was, "Oh."

Meanwhile, I called up a friend from college and started chasing down the leads I had on Chet.

Chapter Twenty-Six

MAE

Thanksgiving dawned cold and clear. The frosty ground crunched under my feet as I walked out to my car. I was meeting my mother for coffee, and the morning felt good. I felt like things were on track for Rowan and me, and I was almost giddy about it. I felt as if I were in a little bubble, and it felt almost too good to be true. A corner of my mind was braced for something to burst.

I hoped maybe, just maybe, we had already done the hard part as far as karma went. At Firehouse Café, while I was waiting for my mom to arrive, I opened up my email. In a mere second, it felt as if I were falling from a great height. My stomach bottomed out, and I felt sick.

So, I heard you told someone what happened.

The email contained a single sentence in the subject line, and it sent me spinning. My skin felt prickly and a sense of panic fisted in my chest. I felt light-headed and saw black dots along the edges of my vision

I knew this feeling well. I'd experienced it way too often during the first few years after it happened.

No, no, no, no!

"Mae?"

My mother's voice broke through the static filling my brain. My heartbeat was still galloping along. It genuinely felt as if I was in true and literal danger at this very moment. But when I looked up into her eyes, I managed to take a breath, and the black dots started to recede. I looked around the familiar café, and Janet's warm laughter reached me where she was talking to a couple at a table nearby.

"Are you okay, honey?" my mother asked after lightly squeezing my shoulder and sitting down across from me.

"Yeah, yeah, I'm fine," I managed.

I tried to marshal my composure and paste something like a polite smile on my face, but I couldn't even do that. I reached for my coffee, and as my hands curled around the mug, I realized they were ice cold. I took a quick swallow, relieved my mother was distracted as she shrugged her coat off her shoulders, letting it fall over the back of the chair, and put her keys in her purse.

When her eyes lifted again, they skated over my face. "What is it?"

I took another swallow of coffee, the warm liquid sliding through that tight, icy fist around my heart. "Why don't you order first?" I heard myself saying

She looked a little puzzled, but the timing was good because Janet happened to stop at our table just then. "Good morning. Mae's already got her coffee, but what can I get for you?" she asked my mother.

"I'll just take a house coffee, no cream and no sugar."

"Do you want anything for breakfast? And what about you, Mae? I think I got distracted after I got your coffee ready," Janet said with an apologetic smile.

I wasn't sure I could eat anything, but I figured I might as well try. My stomach felt empty and sick, almost hollow. "I'll take a plain bagel with butter."

I didn't hear what my mother ordered, but then we were alone, and she looked at me expectantly. Although my timing was terrible, I did something I never thought I would do. I didn't know what I was doing, but I clearly wasn't thinking.

"I never told you this, but someone raped me in college."

My mother's hand flew to her chest, and she gasped. The hiss of it whistled through her teeth as she snapped her mouth shut. She reached across the table, her hand curling over mine. Her touch was warm, and I was still freezing.

"Mae. I'm so sorry. I wish you'd told me before," she said simply.

Oddly, I was calm. The immense relief of simply saying the truth aloud was so profound and strange that this part wasn't stressful. "I don't know why I didn't."

After her initial reaction, I could sense my mother was floundering. "Honey, tell me what happened."

"That's it, that's what happened. It was at a party." My mother blinked. "Someone spiked my drink. That's so common they even have a nail polish for women to use now. I don't go to parties, and I've never accepted a drink from anyone since then," I said, surprised at how calm my voice sounded. I felt weird as if I was watching myself do this and not really in my body.

My mother squeezed my hand. "Why didn't you tell me before? I wish I could've been there for you."

The first wave of emotion hit me—a jumble of sadness and anger and shame.

I shrugged. "I don't know. I'm okay."

"Are you?" she pressed.

"I am."

"I don't even know what to ask. Should I ask questions?" she finally asked after a long pause.

"If you want. I didn't press charges if you're wondering, I did tell some friends and talked to a therapist about it, but that was it."

"Do you want to do something about it now?"

I shook my head slowly. "I don't think so. I looked into it. It would be a difficult case because I'd been drinking, and he drugged me. My memories aren't all that clear."

My mother flinched and took a shaky breath. Just then, the young man who worked with Janet some mornings arrived with my mother's coffee. I was relieved it wasn't Janet. Not because I didn't adore her, but she was way too perceptive. He had a tray full of coffees and plates with food.

"Your food will be out in just a few minutes," he commented just before he moved away to serve the next table.

My mother finally released my hand and lifted her coffee. After a few swallows, she studied me. "What can I do for you?"

"Nothing. I didn't really expect to tell you that, but I guess I just did." I wasn't ready to tell her what prompted this. That stupid email from Chet. Somehow, he knew I had told someone. Well, fuck Chet.

I might be panicking about it, but I wasn't going to keep his dirty secrets. "It wasn't like it was a secret before. I just didn't say anything."

"It breaks my heart that you've carried this alone. I wish I'd known sooner."

I took a gulp of coffee. "It's okay. I honestly don't want to keep talking about it forever. I know it's a shock, and you're trying to absorb the information."

My mother nodded slowly. "It *is* a shock. I want to be there for you. If you don't want to keep talking about it, I understand. Can I ask one more question?"

"Go for it."

"What do I tell your father?"

"You can tell him."

I had abruptly decided this wasn't going to be a secret. I wasn't sure why this shift inside me had happened so fast, but here we were.

"Okay. If he wants to talk to you about it, what should I tell him?"

"That I don't have much more to say other than that. I can tell him exactly what I said to you if that would make him feel better."

My mother sucked in a fast, sharp breath. "Those are all my questions. If you want me to do anything else and support you in any way, please just let me know."

I could sense she wanted to go into comfort mode, but that wasn't what I wanted now. She knew me well enough to know that. I didn't precisely understand why, but I simply wanted the truth out.

"I will."

As if on cue, our breakfast was delivered to the table, effectively ending that conversation. I was still too unsettled to eat much and mostly picked at my bagel. When we were out in the parking lot, my mother gave me a long hug.

"I love you, Mom," I said as she stepped back.

"I love you too. I wish I could have been there for you sooner."

"I know you do. It's okay."

And it *was* okay.

After I climbed into my car, I felt another shock wave, like the ripples from a boulder falling in a pond. A wave crashed over me, and panic started spinning again. I couldn't bring myself to open the email.

Chapter Twenty-Seven

MAE

That night, I arrived at Madison's house. Madison was hosting a Tex-Mex dinner, declaring that winter in Alaska called for her favorite foods. When I arrived, I was pleased to see Phoebe, Susannah, and Maisie there.

Maisie's toddler was bouncing on her lap. I smiled over at the little boy. "He's got your curls."

"He sure does." She lightly tugged a brown curl with her fingers, stretching it out and letting it bounce back before he wiggled off her lap. "Don't worry. He won't be here all night. Beck is coming to pick him up. He's on daddy duty. I told him this was a girls' only night. He's gonna want some of that food," she called over to Madison, who was at the stove.

"I'll make him a to-go plate," Madison called in return.

Madison pulled out a casserole pan of enchiladas, which she'd smothered in cheese and sauce.

"Wow, you're not messing around," I commented.

She flashed a smile. "There's no such thing as too much cheese and sauce."

She pulled out a small round aluminum pie pan and transferred some into it before putting foil over the top. Glancing over at Maisie, she said, "This is for Beck when he gets here."

As if on cue, there was a knock on the door, and Maisie hurried over to answer it. Beck came into the kitchen and glanced around with a grin. "Damn. It smells good in here. I don't get to stay?" he teased when his eyes made their way back to Maisie.

She shook her head. "Definitely not."

Madison approached him, handing over the small pan. "When you get home, just pop this in the oven. It will only need to heat for a few minutes."

"Yes!" Beck flashed a grin, winking at the entire room as he lifted his son into his arms. "Good to see everyone." His gaze landed on me. "Glad you're back in town to stay, Mae."

"Good to be here," I called in return as he waved on the way out.

Maisie sat down across from me, and I eyed her, bemused, as I shook my head. "Honestly, I never would have believed it."

"Believed what?" Maisie prompted.

"That Beck Steele would fall that hard."

Maisie shrugged, her cheeks tingeing pink. "I didn't think so either. Even though I've been in town for years now, I tend to forget how many people grew up with him. He was such a flirt."

"He was," Phoebe chimed in, "but he's always been a nice guy. He was never a jerk."

"Definitely not," I added.

Madison carried the casserole pan over, and we served ourselves using the plates stacked in the center of the table. We chatted casually, covering the usual topics of small-town gossip before Madison eyed

Phoebe. "So, I keep hearing rumors, and I hate being that person."

"It's okay. It's a small town," Maisie offered. "Simply living here is sort of a license to be nosy."

Madison pressed her lips together. "I know, but—"

"I know what you're wondering about," Phoebe interjected. "Yes. My former best friend is engaged to my ex. I broke up with him before I knew about them. I don't want him. I mean, I broke up with him for a reason, but it's totally awkward, and it sucks. To make it even more fun, she's begging for my forgiveness."

"I still can't believe she's trying to do that," I offered.

Phoebe sighed and took a swallow of wine. "Yeah."

"Seriously?" Madison pressed.

Phoebe nodded slowly. "Totally serious. The wedding is here next February."

"Oh my god, really?" Maisie interjected.

"Fuck," Madison offered succinctly.

Phoebe rolled her eyes. "Yeah, that's really all I can think about it."

"What are you going to do?" Susannah asked.

"Well, I'm sure as hell not going to be a bridesmaid in Tasha's wedding like she's asked me."

"I can't even believe that," I repeated.

Phoebe twisted her lips to the side. "She's all, please forgive me, you don't understand, blah, blah, blah, I knew you didn't really love him, and it just happened. I'm glad they're in love. Honestly, I don't want him. I'm not even mad at him. It's here, and I can't do the bridesmaid thing. She sent this long email about it and cc'd my mother on it."

"Your mother?" Madison yelped.

"I know. It's just so embarrassing. I don't know

what to do. Here's something random and weird, though."

"What?" I asked.

"Remember Archer?" Phoebe prompted.

Maisie shook her head. "Obviously, I don't remember. I didn't grow up here."

Madison nodded in agreement.

"Archer Cannon? He was in elementary school with us, right?" Susannah asked.

Phoebe nodded.

Susannah's eyes widened. "Oh, yeah, you two were like best friends."

I nudged Phoebe with my elbow. "What about Archer? He's been gone for years."

"Yeah, he moved after fifth grade, I think. Every so often, I'd hear from him. Anyway, he's moving back to Alaska, and he needs a wife. He asked me."

"I'm sorry, what?" Maisie prompted, leaning forward and resting her elbows on the table.

"Yeah, I know. It's weird. I don't actually know why he needs a wife. Somehow he heard about what happened with my ex and Tasha and thought I might appreciate making it super clear I'm not pining after the guy. I think I'm going to take him up on it," Phoebe explained.

"Seriously?" Susannah asked. "When was the last time you saw him?"

"I think it was fifth grade," Phoebe said. "Maybe it's nuts, but he was my best friend when we were little. I know he's a good guy. It'll just be for this. That's it."

"You're not going to just agree to fake marry some guy you haven't seen in years?" Madison pressed, brushing her long dark hair off her shoulders. I was still getting to know Madison, and I liked her, but her beauty was intimidating.

To make matters even more daunting, she always looked completely put together. For example, she had glittery tips on her fingernails tonight. I was also positive she plucked her eyebrows, yet somehow, they looked natural.

"I'm not ready to say yes yet," Phoebe replied. "Archer said he'll be here in January, and we can talk about it then."

I stared at her. "Um, I think that's a little insane."

"Agreed," Susannah chimed in.

Phoebe shrugged. "Look, my pride is seriously stinging right now. I'm pissed off at Tasha and can't freaking get over how much nerve she has. I'm not going to do anything stupid, but I'm going to talk with him about it when he gets here."

Madison's wide eyes met mine. I glanced back at Phoebe. "Well, I guess you'll figure it out when you do. We'll be here if you need us."

"How are things with you and Rowan?" Maisie asked, a sly glint in her eyes.

"They're good. I think."

"I think it's so freaking adorable. Rowan thought he'd never see you again, and now you're falling in love," Maisie added.

I was in deep when it came to Rowan, and it felt good just to admit it. Except I'd been ignoring that email from Chet. It felt like it was festering in the back of every thought that connected to Rowan. It reminded me of all the time we'd lost.

When I got home that night, I decided to stop ignoring it. I opened up the email in the preview pane, only to realize the subject line was all there was to it. I stared at it, my fingers hovering, almost itching to type out a reply.

I craved the sound of Rowan's voice. But I didn't want to tell him about this, so I didn't call. I never replied to the email.

Chapter Twenty-Eight

ROWAN

"How's it going with Colbie?" Lucas asked.

"Well, she's pissy. But Larry's not talking to her, so she's mad at me, she's mad at my parents, and she's probably mad at you," I replied.

Lucas's startlingly beautiful wife, Valentina, smiled warmly, brushing a red curl off her shoulder. "She'll be all right. Nobody likes to be told who they should or shouldn't see. Eventually, she'll realize he's a jerk."

"I know, but she should have already realized that," I countered.

She pressed her lips together and shook her head. "I'm not your sister, and I didn't date some guy who was a controlling asshole when I was in high school, but I do have super religious parents. They had opinions about everything I should do, and I hated it. Just be patient with her."

Lucas, besotted husband that he was, smiled at her before looking back at me. "She's usually right."

My laugh was dry. "I know she's right. I just hope Colbie eases up on my parents."

Valentina was distracted by their daughter calling

her from the kitchen, and she hurried over, leaving me alone with Lucas.

"It's good to see you," he offered a moment later.

"Good to be here."

"You like living in Alaska?"

"Love it."

"Remy does too," he offered with a nod.

"I know. He'll be staying put since he's married now."

"When do you go back?" Valentina asked as she returned to the room.

At that moment, my sister came in and flounced down on the couch beside me. She smiled over at Valentina. "Hi, how's it going?" She pointedly ignored Lucas.

"Doing well. How are you?" Valentina asked politely as she perched on the armrest of Lucas's chair.

Colbie shrugged. "I'm fine. Did Rowan tell you he has a girlfriend?"

Valentina shook her head. I figured my sister had a point to this, but I decided to wait and see. I didn't have to wait long.

"Yeah, nobody's about to tell him who he can and can't see," Colbie offered with a dramatic eye roll.

Lucas chuckled. "I know you're pissed at us, but I really don't think you want to date a meth dealer."

My sister rolled her eyes. I slid my arm around her shoulders, giving her a quick squeeze. "Ask me before you start seeing someone else."

Colbie's eyes narrowed. "Oh, my god!"

Valentina's words crossed over hers. "You can't do that, Rowan."

"I know, I know," I grumbled. "I just worry about you."

Colbie nudged me with her elbow, and I knew we

were on the way to being okay. After my sister departed, I chatted a little more with Lucas and Valentina.

"You met my friend Mae at UNC, right?"

He nodded. "Oh, yeah, y'all were like besties."

"Yup. We went on a few dates. She's from Alaska. I have to admit, that was maybe more than half the reason I took the job out there."

Valentina's blue eyes held mine. I already knew my cousin's wife was not one to be underestimated, but damn, her gaze was so assessing. I felt as if she peeled back the layers of my soul. "I think you're in love," she announced.

Lucas glanced sideways at her and then back at me, his brows hitching.

"I am," I said simply.

"Are you going to bring her back to visit sometime?" Valentina asked next.

"I hope so," I finally said.

The next day, after brunch with my parents, I called up Darryl again.

After we got through the initial pleasantries, I dived in. "You happen to know how to reach Chet?"

"Dude, I don't think that's a smart idea."

"Why?" I retorted.

"Does Mae know you're trying to reach him? Since you called, Stephanie scouted out a little more info. Mae didn't want to pursue charges back then. One of their friends went with her to talk to the college about it."

"I know but—"

"Come on, Rowan. What are you going to do?"

I let out a frustrated sigh. "Call Chet and, I don't know, make sure he knows I know, and I'll make things difficult for him."

"I get it. I can imagine you want to rip that guy's balls off. He's such a skeevy guy, such a dick, but he's also the kind of guy who would press charges."

"I'm not going to assault him or some dumb shit like that. I'm just gonna call him and let him know he'd better watch his back if I hear that he's done anything like that again."

I could imagine Darryl's eyes rolling, hard. "We can track him down, but I think you should leave it alone unless Mae wants you to do something."

"I'm not going to be stupid, I promise."

An hour later, my phone was practically burning a hole in my hand. As promised, Darryl had texted me a phone number and an email. Chet was living in Raleigh now. He'd transferred to another college and graduated. He worked at some law office. Darryl had sent another text following with the name and phone number of the practice where he worked, suggesting maybe I could just let them know what I knew about Chet.

I stared at the number, but I remembered his warning. I searched out my father in his study. "Dad, you got a minute?"

He only worked part-time now, but he was a lawyer. Years back, he worked for the North Carolina Bar Association.

"You okay?" he asked as I sat down in the chair across from his desk. He closed his laptop and leaned back.

"I'm fine, but I have a question. Hypothetically, suppose someone had a habit of spiking girls' drinks in college and raping them, and went on to become a lawyer. What are the chances the bar association would do anything about that?"

My dad's eyes narrowed. "Is this actually a hypothetical?"

I ran a hand through my hair, letting out a bitter laugh. "No. Remember Mae?"

My dad nodded quickly. "Yeah, your friend from college. I thought y'all might date someday."

"We are now."

His lips started to curve into a smile before his gaze sobered. "Oh, no. Is that what happened to Mae?"

"Yeah, and she's not the only one."

My chest ached and cold anger knotted in my gut every time I thought about what happened to Mae.

"Look, I'm sure you know charges in cases like that are difficult to prove. If enough women come forward, there might be a stronger case. Criminally, the standard is hard to meet unless there's physical evidence. Civil cases are much easier to move forward. I can connect you with a friend of mine who can give you some feedback. Have you talked to Mae about this?"

I shook my head. "Not yet. I was actually going to call the guy who did it and confront him, but I thought better of it and came to talk to you."

My dad stared at me for a long moment, pinching the bridge of his nose before his hand fell to his desk. "I understand why you'd want to call him, but don't do anything stupid. I'm assuming you asked about the bar association because he's a lawyer." At my nod, my father continued, "Unfortunately, people like that are the ones who make a mockery of the legal profession. They misuse and abuse their knowledge."

I swallowed. "I know. I won't do anything stupid, but I'd love to talk to your friend for some feedback about options."

Before I got on my flight that afternoon, I had a

long talk with his friend. Jill clearly reiterated what I already knew. Those cases were difficult to charge under the best of circumstances. With the time elapsed, it would be even more challenging. She also suggested approaching it from the civil side.

As I flew back to Alaska, my mind was churning. I wanted to persuade Mae to do something, *anything*, about this.

Chapter Twenty-Nine

MAE

I couldn't even count how many times I stared at the subject line of that email. I hated the little red dot on the email icon on my phone and my laptop indicating an unread email, but I didn't dare to officially open it. I didn't want Chet to somehow know I'd opened it.

After a last glance at that stupid red dot, I slipped my phone into my purse and hurried through the biting cold air into the airport. Rowan's plane was landing, and it was close to midnight. A light snow was falling outside. I forgot about Chet while I was waiting for Rowan. It had only been six days, and I'd missed him every single minute of every single day.

I waited impatiently outside the security area. I had checked the arrival times to confirm he was due to arrive on time. Restless, I kept checking my watch.

My heart rattled against my ribs the second I saw him. He was tall, standing above the passengers filing out. His eyes landed on mine when he was still behind the glass. My heart felt as if a ray of warm sun shined upon it after days of clouds. Moments later, he was weaving his way through the crowd and stopping in front of me.

"Hey, you," I murmured.

"I missed you," he replied as he folded me in his arms.

His bag slid off his shoulder and thumped to the floor. A sense of relief and peace washed through me. This thing with Rowan was both new and intense but also familiar. He'd been my friend before, and I knew him. I breathed in the scent of him, a little crisp and somehow always with a hint of forest clinging to him. Maybe it was a firefighter thing.

I had no idea how long we stood there until someone bumped into me from behind, apologizing as they moved away.

I lifted my head, leaning up to press a kiss on the underside of his jaw. "My car's warm. Do you need to get anything from baggage claim?"

Rowan leaned over and looped his bag over his shoulder while lacing his fingers through mine with his other hand. "Nope. I hate dealing with baggage claim," he said as he smiled down at me.

I savored the feel of his warm hand around mine. "How was Thanksgiving?" I asked as we walked toward the parking garage.

"It was good. I missed you, but I'm glad I went."

"How's your sister?"

"Well, Colbie's not thrilled with me, but the asshole's not in the picture anymore."

I looked up at him. "What did you do, Rowan?"

"Let's get going, and I'll explain."

A few minutes later, we were in my car, and Rowan's palm was resting on my thigh. After I paid the parking fee and got on the highway, I ordered, "Okay, spill."

"I got the scoop from my cousin Lucas who's on the first responder crew there. The guy she was dating deals meth with his father. His dad has a history of knocking him and his mom around. Colbie's not the first girl he's got a history of being controlling with. I don't know if he ever hit her. She wouldn't tell me, but I suspect he did."

I whipped my gaze to his before looking back at the highway quickly. "That's awful."

"I know. Lucas and I went there and explained we were going to make life miserable for him if he didn't fucking leave her alone. She cried and argued with us about it. It took a few days, but she was speaking to me again before I left."

I glanced his way. "Okay, I understand, but I can imagine Colbie didn't appreciate you being controlling about him."

"Mae, what was I supposed to do? The guy's dealing meth."

"I get it, I do. I just hope she doesn't take it as a reason to push you away."

"I know. I don't think she was happy with him. He's such an ass he told us she sucked in bed. I mean, my god! I don't even want to think about my sister with anyone, but it says a lot about the kind of guy he is that he'd say that to us."

"Sounds like he was just trying to be an ass."

Rowan's voice was dry. "He succeeded. He's got problems with the law, and he doesn't want to be in more trouble than he already is, so here's hoping he stays away from her. I'm pretty sure she didn't see him again after that."

"All you can do is hope for the best. I know I would've been pissed off if someone ordered me around about some guy when I was a teenager."

"Oh, she had that covered, all right." A laugh rustled in his throat.

I squeezed his hand where it rested on my thigh. "Did you have a good Thanksgiving meal?"

"I did, and it was good to see the rest of my family. Tell me how your Thanksgiving was."

"It was small—just my parents and me—but it was nice. I missed you."

"I'm home for Christmas."

Hearing him describe Willow Brook as home set my heart to pounding in my chest. I didn't know why, but I was nervous. This was *a lot*. My feelings about Rowan felt almost too big. We'd known each other so well before when we were friends, and then it all blew up. Now, all the emotions I'd felt before were bombarding me. They were big and deep.

As if he sensed my internal tumult, he squeezed my hand. "Willow Brook is starting to feel like home. But more than that, you're here. And honestly, Mae, home is wherever you are to me."

Oh. My. God. I almost melted right there in the car, but I forced myself to focus. It was snowing out, and I needed to pay attention. We fell into a more relaxed conversation for the rest of the drive.

"Are you tired?" I asked as I turned down the road that led to both of our places.

"I'm tired but wired. That's what travel does to me."

"Do you want me to drop you off at your apartment?"

"Hell no," he said flatly. "Unless for some reason you want to drop me off there."

I shook my head quickly. "Absolutely not."

A few minutes later, we were walking into my house. I was finally starting to call it *my* house.

Sassafras actually came over and greeted Rowan, circling his feet.

"She even let me scratch under her chin," Rowan commented as he glanced over at me.

"I think she likes you."

Rowan cast me a lopsided grin as he straightened and shrugged out of his jacket. "I'll take whatever I can get from her."

"Did you eat on the plane?" I asked as I hung up my coat and toed off my boots.

"I did, but I'm still hungry. Airplane food isn't amazing."

I smiled. "That's why I have a pizza for you. I picked it up earlier and stuck it in the fridge. I figured this way we could just heat it up."

I started to turn toward the kitchen, but he caught my hand and reeled me to him. "This is why I love you," he murmured as he brushed his lips over mine.

My belly shimmied, and my heart pounded hard and fast. "Because I got pizza for you?"

"Yes."

"What do you mean?"

He smoothed a loose lock of hair away from my forehead, tucking it behind my ear and sending shivers chasing down that side of my body. "It's the pizza, but it's not the pizza. It's that you wondered if I would be hungry. It's kind of a small thing, but also a big thing."

"I understand," I whispered right before he kissed me again.

When he lifted his head, his gaze coasted over my face. "Can we have pizza after?" His question came in that low voice, the one that never failed to send butterflies twirling in my belly and liquid need spinning in my veins.

"After what?"

"After this."

He laid another kiss on me, and I forgot about the pizza.

Chapter Thirty

ROWAN

I told myself on the flight home that I would savor Mae and take my time. I was going to have to take a rain check on the savoring because instead, I had her up against the door shuddering as I sank into her silky, clenching core only minutes after we walked inside.

My jeans were shoved down around my hips, and she still had her shirt on. We'd ditched her jeans simply because that was the only way for me to be buried inside her. I held still, resting my forehead against hers for a moment as I took several deep breaths and clung to my control.

"Look at me, sweetheart," I murmured against her lips.

I dragged my eyes open and lifted my head just enough to see her. Her big ginger eyes blinked open, and I could feel the beat of her heart thumping against my chest. We stared at each other. My heart felt so full I thought it might burst.

I loved Mae so much. We didn't say a word. Everything was communicated with our eyes. Her breath hitched in her throat, and I finally drew back, adjusting her in my arms before I filled her again and again and again. Then she was trembling all over, her hips bucking against me. My release took me by surprise, hitting me so hard I let out a rough shout as lightning sizzled through me.

After we disentangled, we changed into more comfortable clothes, and Mae reheated the pizza. We ate in her bed with the TV on in the background. I looked over at her.

"I meant to be smooth about that. It was going to be a whole seduction," I said between bites of pizza.

She grinned. "Seriously?" At my nod, she added, "Okay, I'll hold you to that next time."

I chuckled. I made good on my promise in the sleepy darkness.

When I woke the next morning, Mae was already up. After a quick shower, I found her in the kitchen. She had her laptop open on the kitchen table, and she looked worried. She had that little furrow between her brows, and her nose was scrunched up. She was also tapping her thumb on the counter. That was the give-away. Back in our college days, she'd tap her thumb when she was worried about an exam.

"What is it?" I asked after I'd gotten some coffee and sat down across from her.

Her eyes swung to mine as she took a quick breath as if bracing herself. "Chet emailed me."

I'd been lifting my mug, and it froze in the air. Anger sliced through me like a hot blade. "What?"

She cleared her throat, her face a little pale as she repeated, "Chet emailed me."

I lowered my mug to the table. "About what? How does he even have your email?"

She shrugged. "I don't know. It's just a subject line. It says, 'So, I heard you told someone what happened.' How does he even know I talked to anyone?"

I took a slow breath. "Can I see the email?"

Mae turned her laptop toward me at the table. She stood from her chair, appearing much calmer than me about this. "Don't open it. Just look at it in the preview pane."

My fury had nowhere to go. I wanted to smash her laptop, but that wouldn't do a damn thing to Chet. I wanted to call him and scream, and I had his number. I read the subject line, that hot jolt of fury settling in my gut and churning. She returned to the table a moment later, nudging my mug closer. "Have a sip. It'll help."

I took a quick swallow, the bitter flavor not even doing justice to my mood. "Mae, why didn't you tell me about this? This was days ago."

She lifted a shoulder in a light shrug as she sat down. "What were you going to do? I didn't want to mess up your trip. You had other things to deal with."

I took another gulp of coffee and closed her laptop. "I talked to an attorney."

"What? About this?" She tapped her thumb on the edge of her mug handle.

"Yeah."

Her eyes narrowed. "Rowan, I don't want you to do anything. There's nothing to do."

"Mae, the statute of limitations has not expired," I pressed.

"I know, but it's not a good case. If the attorney told you anything other than that, they're no good. Is that why he's emailing me? When did you talk to the attorney?" She stood from the table abruptly, wrapping her arms around her waist and pacing in a circle in the kitchen.

"Mae, you look more upset about this than the email from Chet." I gestured pointlessly at her closed laptop.

"Because I trusted you."

"Hey, I swear I didn't talk to Chet. I have his number, but I promise he hasn't heard anything from me. I talked to my dad, who put me in contact with a friend of his who handles criminal cases."

She uncurled her arms from her waist, running her hand through her hair and tucking it behind her ears. "I have to get ready for work," she muttered quickly as she glanced up at the clock over the stove.

She didn't even kiss me goodbye. I had a bad feeling, and I had to get to the station. I should've asked her before I talked to anyone. I'd let my own frustration, my need to somehow help, get in the way. I had screwed up.

Chapter Thirty-One

MAE

I kept opening the email on my phone and staring at that stupid subject line. The little red dot was constantly bright on my screen all because of that one email. I was afraid.

Rowan had opened a door I never wanted to open again. I honestly didn't want to pursue anything around this legally. The process alone would eat me alive.

My day was busy at work, but I had plenty of time to think, so I made a decision. I didn't know what to do, but I needed some space. I wasn't blaming Rowan for Chet emailing me, but this was my situation to deal with. I did not want anyone else involved. I just needed to come to my own peace with it. I didn't think closure was possible, if only because the concept was fucking obnoxious for traumatic events.

I was tempted to be a coward and tell Rowan I needed some time via text. But that just didn't feel right. That night, I drove past my house to his apartment, which I'd only been to a few times. We'd fallen into the habit of him mostly staying with me during our short relationship. I was relieved to see his SUV there. We hadn't texted about what we were doing tonight.

My heart gave a sharp twist. Because that was how far and fast we'd fallen into this place of comfort. Now, it felt all blown up emotionally. I didn't need him nosing into this situation. It had been enough for me to share what happened.

I jogged up the stairs on the side and knocked lightly on the door. It swung open only seconds later.

Rowan's alert gaze skated over my face with a searching look. "Hey," he said.

"Can I come in?"

"Of course."

He stepped back and gestured for me to pass by. "I was about to text you and see if you wanted me to come over." His tone was light and casual, although it felt slightly forced.

I stared at him for a long moment. "I'm really upset," I said quietly as I walked past him and stuffed my hands in my pockets.

It said a lot that I didn't even need to explain further. "Mae, I was just trying to help—"

I cut in. "You want to help somehow? I don't need help."

"Oka-aay," he said slowly.

He started to step closer, but I took a step back. "Please don't talk to anybody else about this. Promise me you won't."

"I promise. I won't."

My throat ached, and my chest literally hurt. "I'm afraid, and I need a little time."

"Mae, please," he began, his voice roughened. "Please don't tell me you're going to let this blow us apart. Please. You know I love you."

"I know you do. I love you too, but I just need a few days. That's all."

I didn't even know how to vocalize what I was feeling. This entire situation had somehow shattered the fragile peace I had started to find. There was Rowan and how he connected to my memories of that night long ago that had ripped through my life and sent pieces of me scattering. Then there was the sheer enormity of my feelings for him.

I swallowed and took a shallow breath. "I'll call you when I'm ready."

Turning, I fled back out into the cold darkness. In the few minutes I'd been in his apartment, the snow that had been spitting periodically on my drive home from Anchorage had shifted into an icy sleet. It struck against my cheeks, and I almost welcomed the stinging pain. I couldn't feel the hot tears through it and drove home in a blur.

By the time I got home, there were already several texts from Rowan. I replied with one.

I just need a little time. That's all I'm asking.

Chapter Thirty-Two

ROWAN

"Dude, you look fucking miserable," Remy commented as I walked into the locker room at the station.

I sank onto the bench in front of the lockers. I'd just finished a punishing workout. "I am," I replied with a shrug.

"What gives?" he asked, sitting down across from me.

"I think I fucked up."

"This about Mae?"

I nodded.

"What the hell happened? I thought things were good with y'all."

I took a deep breath, snagging the towel I'd set on the bench beside me and dragging it over my sweaty face.

"Mae wants some time. She's mad at me because —" I paused abruptly, realizing I couldn't even explain the whole situation to Remy. I forged ahead. "I got overprotective, and she didn't appreciate it."

Remy studied me quietly. "I understand that."

"What do you mean?"

"Rachel's ex was really controlling. She's good now, but it was dicey."

"What?" My head whipped up.

He nodded slowly. "Oh, yeah. It's not a secret around town, but it's been a while. She's good, we're good. But I had to learn that it's her past, it's her story. She sets the boundaries on how she manages it. He did jail time, and he's not in town anymore, which makes it a hell of a lot easier. I don't know, though. It would be hard for me if he was around." He eyed me for a long moment. "Is it an ex of hers? He around?"

I shook my head quickly. "Nah, nobody from here. It's college. She asked me not to talk about it. So..."

He dipped his chin. "You have to respect that. I get it. In the end, the details don't matter. You know?"

I shook my head. "What do you mean?"

"As long as she's safe, and she's okay. It's your job to respect whatever boundary she sets around it and be there. It might be different, and she might want you to be more involved if she wasn't safe."

I absorbed that. "What if somebody from her past emailed her out of the blue?"

"Are they here?"

I shook my head quickly.

"Well then, ask her what she wants you to do about it and then do that."

I practically got skid marks from biting my tongue. I wanted to push and ask why, but I knew that wasn't my place. "It's not fucking right that people can do shit and get away with it."

"No, dude, it's not. But it's her world, her past, her story. Not yours. And, trust me, the legal system isn't always an answer. If you want to ask Rachel about it, go for it. Court fucking sucks, and it's brutal. I think it's different when safety is an issue, though. I'm not saying it's your job to call the shots then, but it's a different dynamic, different dialogue."

I took in a deep breath and let it out, leaning back against the lockers. "This fucking sucks. I didn't even know Rachel went through anything like that."

Remy's gaze darkened for a beat. "Oh yeah, her ex knocked her around."

"And he lived right here in town?"

"He doesn't anymore."

"I don't like how many women go through things like that," I finally said.

"Yeah, you and every guy who doesn't think that shit is cool. We've got a long way to go in our world. I don't know the details, and I'm not asking because..." Pausing, he hitched his brows.

I answered his silent prompt. "It's her story."

"Yep."

I let out a sigh. "How was Thanksgiving in NC?" he asked. "Rachel and I are headed there for Christmas. You going back again?"

"Nah. I figure one holiday a year, plus I'm hoping to spend Christmas with Mae."

Remy gave me a considering look. "Well, then you're gonna have to give her that time she asked for."

"I know." I stood from the bench. "I'm gonna go shower."

He clapped me on the shoulder as I walked by. I let the steaming water pound down over my tired muscles, wondering what to do. I was an action guy. Waiting didn't sit well with me. Chet's phone number was burning a hole in my phone, but I knew doing anything about that would only make things worse.

Chapter Thirty-Three

MAE

Phoebe studied me from across the table at Firehouse Café. "What's up?" she asked, cocking her head to the side.

"I told Rowan I needed some time, and I'm cranky about it," I said honestly.

"What for? You two were all lovey-dovey."

"I know."

I thought for a minute about whether I wanted to tell her the whole messy story. I decided I might as well confide in someone because the few people who knew what actually happened aside from Rowan were my college friends. I'd shoved it down into the memory banks after that.

"Did I ever tell you why we stopped being friends to begin with?" I asked, even though I knew the answer.

Phoebe shook her head slowly. "You were pretty vague."

"I kind of freaked after I became a statistic."

"A statistic?"

"Yep. Rowan's roommate spiked my drink and

raped me. I couldn't deal, so I just cut off all contact. I'm a college sexual assault stat."

Phoebe's hand flew to her chest, her eyes going wide with her gasp. "Oh, my god, Mae. I'm so sorry. Are you okay?"

I felt strangely calm, just as I had when I told my mother. Although, my body felt a little tingly, almost like static. "Yeah. I think so."

"What does this have to do with you and Rowan now? He didn't take that guy's side or anything?" A look of horror crossed her face.

"Oh, god, no! I didn't even tell him back then. They weren't close. None of the guys liked him, so Rowan and his other friends got another place after that semester."

"What does this have to do with him now?" she repeated. "Does Rowan know what happened?"

I swallowed and nodded. "Yeah. It's weird. I got this email from Chet, and then Rowan talked to his dad and an attorney about it when he was back in North Carolina. It feels—" I sighed. "I don't, I don't even know how to explain. I don't want... I actually..." I kept stuttering over my own words, frustrating myself. "Back when it happened, I did go talk to the campus sexual assault team about it. They were nice, but they explained that the case would be really difficult to pursue since I didn't remember much. I decided then not to do anything about it, and I don't want to open it back up now. I just want to move on. I'm upset that Rowan talked to somebody about it without asking me."

Phoebe studied me quietly for a moment. "I get it," she finally said. "I really do. It's yours to figure out. But I'm going to go out on a limb here and suggest that maybe rather than cutting him out, you let him know you need him to respect how you feel about it going forward. That's always an option."

My heart literally ached in my chest. "I know that's an option." I twisted a napkin between my fingers. "Then there's that stupid email. I don't know what to do about that."

"Tell that asshole to fuck off. Do *not* let this guy have power over you. Maybe you're not going to take him to court, but what the fuck? Do you really think it's because Rowan talked to somebody? I mean, how would this guy even know about that? That doesn't make sense."

"It's weird. I don't understand how he knows I talked to anyone."

Phoebe nodded firmly. "Yeah, it's fucking weird and creepy and intimidating. I'm sure that's his point. Maybe you don't want anything to happen about the past and I get that, but don't let this guy fuck with you from a distance like that."

"I don't know what to do, though." I shrugged, hating the sense of helplessness elicited by a mere email.

My friend, a tough as hell hotshot firefighter and who probably had way more nerve than me, pursed her lips. "If you don't want to do anything, then I say just block him and go from there. You're probably not going to hear any more from him. Or reply and ask him. What's the worst that could happen?"

My stomach flipped over. I stared at her. "Uh, I don't know."

"You're here in Alaska. He's not going to show up here. Like, that's crazy. He has far more to lose than you do."

"Except for my peace of mind. That's why I didn't

want Rowan to talk to anyone about it without asking me. He just went and did that."

"This guy's email has already fucked with your peace of mind. I also can't help but wonder if you're upset with Rowan because he's safe to be upset with."

"What do you mean?" Now, my stomach churned uncomfortably. Not out of fear but a sense of doubt.

"I mean, you can't do a damn thing about the past, but you can do something about now. It's not okay that Rowan went all manly helpful, but he is someone you can react to now. He does respect you, so you can be upset, and it's safe."

"Oh." I eyed her.

"Let's do it together."

"Do what together?"

Phoebe shrugged casually, her attitude all no-big-deal. "Reply to that email."

My heart was pounding in a reckless, sick beat. Suddenly, I realized something. I was letting Chet's email get to me. Fuck him.

"Okay, what do we say?"

"Type it in your notes first. Don't just hit reply."

"Always smart," I replied with a firm nod.

Phoebe scooted her chair around to my side of the table, offering, "Don't obsess over it. Just say something direct and blunt."

"Uh, okay." I pulled up my notes.

After a little tinkering with Phoebe reviewing the final product, I replied, *"I can talk to whoever I want. Don't fucking email me again and leave me alone. If you don't, I might pursue my legal options."*

I looked over at Phoebe. "You really think I should send this?"

She nodded vigorously. "Hell fucking yes! I know

that red dot is driving you crazy, isn't it? It's the only unopened email you have."

"Yeah, it's driving me nuts." I rolled my eyes.

She laughed. "Just do it."

Phoebe's courage and direct approach were infectious. I finally felt like I wasn't letting this hold my emotions hostage anymore. I opened his email, pasted in my reply, and hit send before I could think any further about it.

"Now block his email, and it'll go into your trash. If you decide to open it, you can, but it won't give you the red dot," she offered matter-of-factly.

"I freaking hate those!" I burst out laughing.

Phoebe grinned over at me just as a server stopped by to ask if we wanted more coffee. Once he moved on, I looked over at her. "Enough about me. How are you doing with the whole wedding thing?"

"Well, that was a quick shift."

I waved my hand in the air. "I'm fine. I really don't want to dwell on that. I swear. We dealt with my thing."

She eyed me skeptically. "First, what are you going to do about Rowan?"

"Ugh! I haven't decided. I need a little more time to think about it. We're not done, I swear. Now..." I paused and hitched my brows. "Let's talk about what the hell you're going to do about Tasha's wedding."

She drummed her fingertips on the table. "Nothing. There's nothing I can do. I'm not going to be her bridesmaid, though, and I already told her."

"Good for you. Honestly, I still can't believe she had the nerve to ask. When is the wedding?"

"Valentine's Day," she ground out.

"Oh, my god. You're fucking kidding me. Valentine's Day?"

"Yeah. She said she wanted a winter wedding." Phoebe wrinkled her nose at that.

"Who does that?"

"Does what?"

"Marry their ex-best friend's ex in their hometown on freaking Valentine's Day," I said flatly.

"My former friend when she's trying to rub it in."

"Are you sure you're over your ex?" I pressed.

Phoebe let out a heavy sigh. "Yes, I really am. I thought about breaking it off for months before I did. But this sucks. He was screwing around on me with the person I thought was my best friend."

"I know, I know. It's so shitty."

"Every time I think about it, I get angry. And then, I get angry with myself for being angry because I shouldn't care. Like, I don't want to be with him, but I can't get over what she did."

"Oh, it's a *huge* violation of trust. Tasha broke a key friend rule. It's totally not cool to screw around with your friend's fiancé. That she asked you to be in the wedding is next-level crazy. I'm sure we can rustle up a collective town refusal to attend the wedding. It can just be her and her parents," I offered.

Her hair swung around her shoulders as she shook her head swiftly. "No, no. I don't want to do that."

"What are you going to do about Archer?"

"I'm trying to figure that out."

"Have you seen him yet?"

"Nope. Apparently, he's coming to town right after Christmas."

"Well, that is going to be an interesting conversation. I can't wait to hear about it."

After the crew finished up a training exercise, Graham invited us to go out for drinks. I was in no mood to go. It had been five days since Mae and I last spoke. Every fucking day I drove by her house and had to keep my hands from turning the steering wheel into her driveway. It sucked. Big time. I missed her every day.

Even though I was in no mood, I went because I needed the distraction. Otherwise, I'd have been my apartment all alone and be cranky as hell.

"Rowan, you've been around a lot lately," Alex commented the following day as I brushed snow off my windshield.

His truck was parked beside my SUV. I glanced over, ignoring his observation and asking, "How come you don't use the actual garage?"

"Because there's room for one car, but the other half is filled with my stuff," Delilah called over as she approached us. He chuckled as she stopped beside him. "I promised him my Christmas present would be me going through it and deciding what I don't want to keep."

Alex shrugged easily as he caught her hand and reeled her to him for a quick kiss. "I don't mind. This is the first place I've owned that had an actual garage. I'm used to winter without parking in a garage, so I can survive."

"I know, but you're being all manly and insisting I park in it." Delilah glanced over at me and rolled her eyes. "I try parking outside, and then he just starts my car and drives it into the garage."

I smiled at them. "Enjoy it," I offered.

"How's Mae?" Delilah asked next.

I narrowed my eyes at her as I opened the passenger door and tossed the snow brush on the floor. "Delilah, I didn't take you for a gossip," I replied as I straightened and closed the door.

"I'm not gossiping. I'm just asking how Mae is because that's where you usually stay," she said pointedly.

I let out a sigh. "We're working some things out. Do you know her well?"

"Not really. I'm still getting to know people around here, although you're newer than me in town so now I feel like old news," Delilah replied lightly.

Alex opened the passenger door to his truck and gestured her in. "I know Mae pretty well. We grew up together. Do I need to kick your ass or something?"

"Fuck, no. I swear I didn't do anything," I insisted.

Then I thought about my conversation with Remy and how I'd talked to that attorney without asking Mae about it. I was trying to believe I hadn't crossed too many lines. "I wouldn't deliberately hurt Mae."

Alex gave me a considering look as he closed the passenger door. "I'd guess you're in love."

"Hey, you don't even need to guess. I'm in love," I said flatly.

Alex chuckled. "Well then, you'd best figure things out in a hurry."

"I'm working on it."

A few minutes later, I drove by Mae's house again. I wanted to see her so much it was a visceral ache in every corner of my body. I missed her like crazy.

I wanted to know how the hell Chet knew she had talked to anybody because I knew nobody I talked to would've said a word to him. Once I was on the highway, I tapped my screen to make a call.

Darryl answered on the third ring with, "What's up?"

I cut right to my point. "It's a little weird, but Chet actually ended up emailing Mae. Somehow, he knows she talked to someone. I know you wouldn't have said anything, but I was wondering if you might know."

"What the fuck?" my friend muttered. "Hang on, let me ask Steph." I heard him move the phone away and call out his wife's name.

A minute later, she was on the line. "I've got you on speaker," he explained and quickly summarized what I'd just told him. "What do you think?"

"That's weird. I have my suspicions, though," Stephanie said.

"You do?"

"So, when that happened," she began.

My gut churned just thinking of it. That singular event had burned a line through my friendship with Mae. Just when I thought our relationship was finally going to the next level, it had been severed completely. Except it had never been severed in my heart.

"Rowan?" Stephanie prompted.

"Sorry," I said quickly. "I'm driving and was making sure I didn't miss an exit."

"Chet still lives in Raleigh. I'll need to ask around,

but Mae told us at the time, right after it happened. I went with her down to the clinic. It was stressful and weird. She decided she didn't want to pursue charges because she didn't remember much. She was just so freaked out, she couldn't connect the dots. But there was a girl who happened to be at the clinic that day, and I think she heard part of the conversation. She lived on our same floor at the dorm and not a single one of us trusted her. She was with a guy at the time who was buddies with Chet."

"But what does that have to do with now?" I asked, genuinely puzzled.

"Chet took a job in Raleigh at a law firm where that woman works. Maybe he just found out she said something back then."

I turned that over in my mind. The whole thing was bothering me, and more than anything, I was fucking furious about the whole situation. I was really, *really*, resisting the urge to swoop in, call Chet, and tell him to fuck off. I was also ignoring a message from that attorney who had nicely followed up, likely as a favor to my father, to see if Mae wanted to talk with her.

"Tell me what you find out," I said to Stephanie.

"Of course. Also, tell Mae I said hey," she replied.

"You got it."

"We kind of lost touch after I had kids." Darryl's chuckle was wry at that comment. "It's a sad side effect of being a mom. You finish college, and life goes on."

"I'll make sure to tell her you said hey. She's got the same number, you know."

"How about this? You let her know I said hey, and then I'll text her. I don't want it to be weird."

"You got it. And thanks for trying to chase this

thing down with Chet. I appreciate it," I said sincerely.

After the call, my heart gave a sharp twist. Stephanie assumed Mae and I were all good. And we weren't. Mae was frustrated with me for nosing into things, and I'd just gone and done it again. I pounded my fist lightly on the steering wheel. Mae hadn't told me I couldn't text her, so I could at least do that. Maybe she didn't even care why Chet emailed her out of the blue, but I did, and I did *not* fucking trusting that guy.

After stopping to get some coffee, I decided a call to my father was in order. When I wasn't sure what to do, he usually gave good advice. He answered immediately because he always did when he was available.

"Hey, Dad."

"Hey, Rowan, how's it going?'

"How's Colbie?"

I could hear the smile in his voice. "Well, she'd win an award for being cranky, but she isn't trying to get back with that guy. Whatever you and Lucas told him, he's steered clear. He also managed to piss her off."

"Well, that is good. What pissed her off?"

"Apparently, he started spreading rumors about her."

"He's a fucking asshole. Excuse my language," I replied.

"Sometimes it's the only thing that expresses something properly," my father offered blandly. "Anyway, she's back to being a firecracker. It's good to have her back, rather than sullen and hiding from everything and not talking to us. She's even slamming her door again."

I chuckled. "Ah, well, then we know she's good. After you and I finish chatting, I'd love to talk to her."

"You got it. So, what are you calling about?"

I quickly filled him in on the situation with Mae, commenting at the end, "Your friend told me it's not a great case, so I'm going to leave it alone unless Mae wants to do something."

"Trust me, the police know those stories, and we know they're true. But our legal system isn't like television. Nothing happens fast. When there's no physical evidence, testimony is key. So, it'd be her word against his. Beyond a reasonable doubt is a high standard to meet under the best of circumstances."

"I know." I took a swallow of my coffee, tracing the top of the lid after I set it in the cup holder in the console.

"I know you want to fix this for her. But you've got to let this be her call. I know it's hard. Our world is weird. Being a man isn't about being the tough guy and calling the shots. It's about being strong enough to let whoever you love make their own decisions about things that really matter. This is something that really matters." My dad's voice was low and solemn.

My chest felt tight, and I had to swallow through the thickness in my throat. "I know you're right."

"I know you do. By the way, your sister walked in for the last half of that conversation so she's gonna want to know what it's about. Call anytime. I love you."

"Love you too, Dad."

And then, my sister was on the phone, immediately opening with, "What in the hell was that about?"

I opened my mouth to tell her to back off with the swearing but chuckled instead. "Never mind."

"Hell is a place, you know," she teased. "Seriously, what's Dad talking about?"

Fuck my life. Now, my sister was asking, and I

didn't feel like I could tell her the whole story. The best I could do was summarize and not mention Mae's name. "Here's the deal: a woman who I care about had something happen to her. I might have tried to do something about it, and she didn't appreciate it."

"Oh, you mean like you did with my boyfriend?" She threw that question like a gauntlet.

"Yes, like that," I replied honestly. "But you're not eighteen, so it's a little different."

Colbie was quiet for a few beats before she spoke. "Here's the thing: even if you're right, it still sucks. Like, Larry was an asshole, and he was getting controlling. I did figure that out, and I'm grateful for you and Lucas getting all like tough because he was doing some serious shit and it was happening right now. But if this was even a year later, and you tried to nose in my business when something was already over, I'd be pretty upset."

I went quiet this time. "Okay, so it's okay that we nosed in your business?"

"Well, yeah. Because he was dealing meth, and I didn't realize that. That's dangerous, and I was in a bad situation with him. He hadn't hit me yet, but he was getting there."

"Are you fucking kidding me?" I growled.

"Fuck is way worse to say than hell," Colbie said sharply.

I took a breath, letting it out slowly. "So, you're really going to stay away from this guy?"

"Yes, I am, but it doesn't mean I'm always going to make the right decisions. I don't even know what you're talking about because you're not telling me very many details. I'm assuming that's because you're trying to be respectful, but I hope you get my point."

"I think I do," I said slowly.

"I would have liked to have been able to figure it out myself. But—"

I couldn't help but cut in. "Larry was into some criminal things."

"Fine, he was," she muttered. "It was a different situation, and it was happening right now. All you can do is help someone get safe, but once they're safe, well, the rest is their call."

"Wisdom from my sixteen-year-old sister," I offered dryly.

"You don't have to listen, but you were right about Larry, and I can admit it. Maybe you should listen to me. I have a point."

"I know you have a point," I said softly. "I'm glad you're okay."

"I'm getting there. Now, I gotta go because my friend's texting me. I love you."

"I love you too."

I turned into the parking lot at work, sitting in the car for a few minutes to gather my thoughts. Lifting my phone, I typed out a text to Mae. I hit send and hoped she'd reply before the end of the day.

Chapter Thirty-Five

MAE

Rowan: *I figured something out. I know you're right, and I'm hoping we could talk tonight.*

I stared down at Rowan's text, my lips curling into a smile. I missed him a lot, enough that it hurt. And we did need to talk. I didn't need any more time away from him, and I also wanted his feedback. I typed out a reply.

Me: *Why don't you come over tonight? I'll make dinner. Also, I think Sassafras misses you. I should be home by 4:30ish. You can come over whenever you want. It's supposed to snow, so don't be out late.*

I laughed as I hit send. I was pretty sure Rowan could handle himself in the snow.

I stopped by the grocery store after work. I was planning to make an old favorite of ours from college. Like many college students, we'd been just getting by when it came to money. We ate a lot of ramen noodles, straight out of those crinkly packages. I'd decided to teach myself how to make it one night. We'd promptly discovered homemade ramen was *waayyyy* better than the kind from the packages. But with being busy college students, we never had enough time, so we'd only made it twice. The first time, and then I'd made it for our very first dinner date. That was also the night of our very first kiss.

After I got home, I started prepping dinner. Sassafras was super curious about anything I did in the kitchen. She liked to watch me from her perch on the windowsill. She seemed to understand she wasn't supposed to get on the counter, which was kind of surprising because usually, she did whatever she wanted.

When I heard the knock on the door, I turned the burner down, practically sprinting from the kitchen into the living room to open the door. It had only been five days.

Rowan was standing there, and the snow was falling around him. I stood frozen in place for a few beats before he prompted, "Can I come in?"

"Oh!" I leaped back.

Closing the door behind him, I watched as he hung up his jacket and toed off his boots. He ran a hand over his hair, which was damp from the snow. We stood there for another moment, and I felt silly.

"Come 'ere," he murmured.

A second later, he folded me into his arms. I took a deep breath, relaxing for the first time in days.

"How are you?" he asked as he stepped away.

"I'm good." I curled my hand around his, giving him a light tug. "Come watch me cook."

Sassafras had followed me out to the living room and eyed Rowan suspiciously from the armrest of the closest chair. Rowan scratched under her chin as he walked by.

When we walked into the kitchen, he commented, "Smells good. What are you making?"

I smiled up at him. "Ramen."

His brows hitched up, a smile slowly curling his lips. "This will be the first time I've had homemade ramen since the last time you made it for me."

"Seriously?"

He nodded. "You're the only person who ever made it homemade for me. It's kind of trendy now, I think."

"I got your favorite beer," I offered as I dropped his hand and strode to the refrigerator to open it.

"What's my favorite beer?"

His eyes were warm, and my belly shimmied.

"I got that kind you like from the brewery in Anchorage. It's hip." Rowan chuckled. "Sit." I gestured to the table.

"Oh, you're gonna wait on me?" he teased as he sat down.

"Sort of. I'm just waiting for the ramen to finish simmering."

"Are you going to have a beer?" he asked.

"I'll have some wine. You can have wine if you prefer."

"Beer is always my preference."

I fetched him a beer and poured a glass of wine for myself before sitting down across from him. I felt nervous, but I wasn't sure why. I suppose I just needed to spit it all out. I opened my mouth to talk, but he interjected. "Can I say something first?"

I went still and stared at him before replying, "Of course."

My heartbeat started to strum a little faster.

His eyes bored into mine, and he cleared his throat. "You were right, but I didn't understand."

"What do you mean?" I whispered.

"I wanted to do something about what happened

with Chet, or rather what Chet did, but that's not my place at all. Whatever happens is your decision, and I should've respected that. I just felt so helpless and so angry. I understand why you got upset with me."

He fell quiet as emotion rushed through me. I took a shuddery breath. I wanted to cry, and tears stung my eyes.

Rowan's eyes widened. "Mae, I didn't mean to upset you," he said hoarsely.

I shook my head quickly. "I'm not upset. I'm just emotional. Thank you for understanding." A part of me wanted to apologize for getting upset with him. But it was important for me to be able to simply hold to that.

I opened my mouth, my habit to apologize for making any man uncomfortable, almost overriding my feelings, but I snapped it shut quickly.

"What were you about to say?" he pressed.

"In a way, I want to say I'm sorry I got upset, but it is really important. It's also not really about you. It's just important to me that I be able to... to manage this, I guess. I don't want to pursue anything legally at all. I want to be able to just let it go. I know trying to do anything about it now isn't going to solve anything. It's really not. I thought about it a lot, and I looked into it again after we talked."

"What do you want to do about him emailing you?" he asked quietly.

I met his eyes. "I already replied."

His brows flew up, and his eyes widened with alarm. "Mae, why—"

I held a palm up. "It's fine. He can't do anything to me. He can't. I basically told him to fuck off, and that if he reached out to me again, I might pursue my legal options. And if he does, I might do that. I didn't do it by myself. I was with Phoebe, and I got sick of staring at the red dot on my phone."

I could see the muscles in his jaw clench. He took a deep breath, his shoulders rising with it, as he leaned his head back and closed his eyes. He let it out with a sigh when he leveled his gaze with mine again. "This isn't easy for me."

"What?" I pressed.

"I have his number. I want to fucking call him and tell him to go straight to hell. I'd also like to kick his ass."

"Please don't. Just don't open that door, Rowan."

"I haven't, and I won't," he said somberly.

"I think you should delete the number from your phone." I could tell he didn't like that suggestion.

"Why?"

"Because if you don't, it's going to burn a hole in your phone and tempt you. If I change my mind and I want to track him down later, we can get his number one way or another. In the world of the internet, it's not that hard to find someone even when they don't want to be found."

"I know but—" he began to protest.

"Rowan, this is important to me." I held my hand out.

Muttering something indecipherable, he slipped his phone out of his pocket and pulled up the number. I watched as he hit delete. "You promise you'll tell me if you change your mind." His eyes lifted to mine again.

"Absolutely. Look," I reached for his hands across the table. The moment we touched, relief coursed through me. This was Rowan. We'd reconnected and finally built on that friendship that had been so important to me once before. "You're my best friend. You were before, and you are again."

"I hope I'm more than your friend," he said quietly.

"You know you are. I love you, and I love that you're protective of me. But you know what?" He cocked his head to the side. "In the movies and in books, there's a perfect happy ending where it's tied up with a bow. If there's a bad guy, he goes to jail. And maybe that will happen for Chet someday, but it won't change the past. It's not going to help me to chase him down. It's not. I wish there was some kind of way for me to know that he would never do it again. I just feel relieved he had to leave the school because of my report and someone else's. That's the most I can hope for."

"Mae." My name was a ragged whisper.

"Rowan, you know there's not much else that will happen. Maybe the world will change, and things will get better. But the world we live in now is one where somebody made a nail polish to prevent what happened to me because it's *that* common."

His palms were warm as he squeezed my hands. "It's not fair."

"I know it's not fair. I really do."

He studied me quietly before nodding slowly.

"Can we stop talking about it now?"

He swallowed and nodded again. "We're sure not going to solve it tonight."

"I know you like to fix things, so I know how hard it is for you to step back and let this be something I figure out. If I want your help fixing it, I'll tell you, but I'm okay. That's what matters."

We did actually manage to move on from that dreaded topic. That was a miracle in and of itself for me. Back when I'd severed my friendship with Rowan in college, I'd believed I'd never be able to think about Rowan without getting all caught up in my head about what happened with Chet. Life and Rowan had proved me wrong because Chet was a footnote in the early part of our story. I refused to let it be anything more. We had so much more to our life together.

We had ramen, and it was delicious. Then I got to fall asleep beside him again.

Afterward, he helped me string Christmas lights in the living room and promised me that the next day, no matter how cold it was, he would hang them on the outside of the house.

Even though I only meant for us to watch television and snuggle, I somehow ended up tracing my hands over his chest and straddling him. I was too greedy, and I'd missed him so, so, *so* much. Before I knew it, we were half undressed, and I was rising up over him as he filled me. The glittering lights cast a shimmer over his face as his hands pressed into my hips, and he brought me to a shattering climax.

Chapter Thirty-Six

ROWAN

The two weeks that passed before Christmas were some of the best weeks of my life. When things finally fell into place for Mae and me, I was flooded with joy. Facing what I had to fight against—to let her handle things the way she needed to—was intensely uncomfortable for me. Yet it opened up a doorway in our intimacy, taking it to a deeper level. As painful as it was to absorb what happened, we were able to build on the foundation of our friendship.

Willow Brook around Christmas was beautiful. Snow glittered under the sun on the mountaintops, and the evergreen trees were dusted with white. The landscape was all winter wonderland.

The very weekend after we made up, I even managed to finish getting that hideous shag carpet out of Mae's house. Life was feeling just plain good, the kind of good that felt solid and stable. I hadn't even known I craved that feeling, but I did.

I passed on Stephanie's message to Mae, and they'd texted back and forth a few times. It was a small thing, but I was glad Mae had reconnected with her.

One evening, after a training exercise at work, I was getting out of the shower at Mae's house, and she called my name.

"You need something?" I asked. I walked down the hallway in my jeans, dragging the towel across my damp chest.

"I think that attorney's calling you." She pointed at my phone where I'd left it on the counter.

Glancing down, I read where the screen flashed *NC Attorney*. I lifted my eyes to hers. "Should I ignore it?"

"Answer it. Let's see what she has to say. Any idea why she'd be calling you?"

I shrugged. I genuinely didn't know. Christmas was three days away, and I didn't want to ruin it.

Mae nodded encouragingly when I raised my eyes to hers in question. I lifted my phone, swiping my thumb across the screen.

"Hello?"

"Hi, Rowan. I know we left it that you would call me if your friend wanted to follow up, but I had some information," Jill explained.

"Oh, do you mind if I put you on speaker? Mae's with me."

Mae had been stirring something on the stove. Pausing, she turned the flame under the burner down, then shifted to face me.

The attorney replied, "Of course not."

Once I had the phone on speaker, I held it between Mae and me, offering, "My girlfriend, Mae, can hear you now."

"Oh, hello, Mae," Jill said politely. "I had an interesting piece of information that I wanted to share."

"What's that?" I asked.

"I did a little digging, and, apparently, the perpetrator didn't report the situation with the college on his bar application, which is a requirement. This guy had official consequences at the university. I didn't want to do anything without your permission, but we do have the option to report that to the bar. Maybe it's not the same as a legal case, but the bar association records are public information. What do you think?"

Mae and I stared at each other. I could tell she was anxious. She held a slotted spoon in her hand, and her fist was clenched tightly around it. My heart felt caught tight in a vise. I reached over, curling my hand around her arm and sliding it down. Her eyes lifted to mine as she uncurled her hand from the spoon and set it on the counter.

She took a shaky breath before replying, "I think that's a good idea. Does it involve anything from me?"

"Not at all. You and someone else reported him to the college, and he wasn't allowed to return the following semester. The college has a disciplinary record. While they can refuse to release the report, he's required to disclose the status of it on his bar application. I can take it from here if you're okay with that."

Mae swallowed. "I am. Would you mind updating me?

"Of course not. Should I call you directly, or should I contact Rowan? Whatever is most comfortable for you," Jill said.

"Either is fine. Let me give you my phone number."

The attorney took down Mae's phone number, then she wished us happy holidays, and we ended the call.

When I met Mae's gaze, I wasn't sure how to read her expression. "Well?" I prompted.

I slid my hand down to curl around hers.

"That actually feels right." I opened my mouth to say something, and she held a finger up. "I know you don't think it's enough. And in a way, maybe it isn't. But I would be a terrible witness in a court case, Rowan. I honestly don't remember much of it clearly."

"He drugged you, Mae," I said, my throat aching with every word.

"I know. It's just not that simple. Maybe if more women come forward, there can be some kind of combined case, and I would testify in that. This is enough. It's not right that he lied on his bar application. I don't even know how he would think that was okay. He might as well have some kind of consequence, other than not being able to return to school." She shook her head slowly, her lips twisting. "You know, you read about this in the news. But, wow, our world lets some people off really easy."

"I know," I said quietly.

"With this, it's also way better that I don't have to do anything."

"And if he tries to email you or call you?" I pressed.

"If he tries that, you can talk to him."

"Are you really okay?"

Mae nodded. "I hate that it happened, and I hate what it did to us, but I'm really okay."

"If you're okay, then I'm okay."

Her eyes held mine, and she leaned up, pressing a soft kiss on the underside of my jaw. "We have a thing to do on Christmas Eve," she said when she stepped back.

"We do?"

"Dinner with my parents."

"Apparently, there's a thing at the fire station too. I don't have the details."

"Oh, we can do both." Mae smiled up at me.

"You sure?"

"Yeah, my parents are old. They want to have dinner at five."

I chuckled. "We can handle dinner at five and then head to the fire station."

EPILOGUE

Mae

Christmas Eve dawned clear and icy cold. Sunny days in Alaska in the winter tend to be the coldest. The sun cast bright shards of light across the landscape, and icy stalks of dead grass glittered. I wrapped a scarf around my neck and tugged my hat on before I stepped outside.

Rowan had to go into the station this morning, and he'd already warmed up my car. I smiled to myself. When I stopped in at Firehouse Café, Phoebe was sitting at a coffee table with a man I didn't recognize. She waved me over.

"Hey, do you remember Archer?" she asked when I stopped beside the table.

I looked over at the man in question. "Archer Cannon?" This man was something all right. He had burnished gold hair and almost silver eyes. The only way to describe his face was chiseled, which felt ridiculous, but it was the only word that came to mind.

He smiled. I was deeply in love with another man, but I knew that smile did something to plenty of women. "You don't look anything like little Archie in fifth grade, although you do have the same hair and same eyes," I offered.

He chuckled. "Good to see you, Mae."

When I glanced toward Phoebe, her cheeks were tinged pink.

"What brings you back to Willow Brook?" I asked. "Do you have any family still here?" I didn't think his parents were around, but I didn't know if he had other family nearby.

"You remember the Cannon Mine?"

"I do. It closed, like forever ago. Aren't they trying to re-open it?" I replied.

Archer dipped his chin in acknowledgment, and even that was kind of sexy. I flicked my eyes to Phoebe, thinking she would have one hell of a time resisting this guy.

"It did close, but my family owns it. I'm here to take over management."

"Isn't there a big thing about the environment with that? I've only been back a month or so and am getting caught up on all the local issues, but unless I'm confused, there's a ton of opposition to re-opening it."

Archer nodded slowly. "Don't worry, we're not going to ruin the environment. That's why I'm here."

Phoebe cast him an assessing look. "Here's to hoping."

"Well, it's good to see you. I've got a few errands to run after getting coffee. Welcome back to Willow Brook."

Archer smiled again. "Good to see you, Mae."

"Are you bringing him to the fire station tonight?" That question slipped out without me thinking.

Phoebe looked a little flustered, which was definitely *not* a Phoebe thing. She was a badass hotshot firefighter. She didn't do flustered.

"She didn't mention it," Archer offered with a sly grin. "But I'd love to go."

Feeling mischievous, I replied, "Oh, you should totally go. I'll be there with Rowan."

I was certain Phoebe would have glared at me if it weren't for Archer sitting right there. I grinned and patted her lightly on the shoulder. "See you tonight."

As planned, we went to my parents' house for an early dinner. I was returning from the bathroom and found my father with his hand on Rowan's shoulder. Their heads were bent close together as they conferred. My mother sat beside my father, smiling almost giddily.

"What's going on?" I asked when I reached the table.

"Nothing," my mother said quickly, too quickly.

I knew she was hedging, but whatever. "You two enjoy the staff holiday party at the fire station," my father said a few minutes later.

"We will. Good to see you both," Rowan replied as he reached for my hand.

"What was that about?" I asked once we stepped out into the freezing cold night.

"Nothing, just chatting with your parents," he replied casually.

"That wasn't nothing," I retorted.

"Wasn't that a double negative?" Rowan teased.

I rolled my eyes. "Fess up."

"You're going to have to wait."

"What if I don't want to wait?"

All I got was a low chuckle in return. I contemplated badgering him on the drive to the fire station, but it was only about three minutes. When we arrived, we were swept into the back area. I glanced around. "Wow, it's festive."

Maisie appeared at my side. "Isn't it, though? I even made the guys help me decorate," she said solemnly.

Beck arrived at her side, adding, "And we did a great job."

Susannah strode over, pulling me into a quick hug. "Hey, you! Glad you two could make it."

"Wouldn't miss it. This place is bigger than I expected." The utilitarian space was decorated with some small wreaths, and glittering lights hung from the ceilings with large red bows in the corners of the room. There was a table with plenty of alcohol and a collection of food.

"You didn't tell me it was a potluck," I said, nudging Rowan in the side.

His eyes caught mine as he smiled sheepishly. "I told them that we had to go to dinner with your parents, and I didn't have time. I didn't want to make it your responsibility."

I sighed. "Ugh. We're that couple now."

"What couple?" Graham asked as he approached with Madison's hand in his.

"The couple who didn't bring anything to the potluck because Rowan didn't tell me," I explained.

"He said you had to have dinner with your parents tonight," Graham replied.

"Well, we did, but I would've made cookies or something. Anything."

Madison shrugged. "It's okay. You can bring something next time."

There were enough friends here that I forgot to

wonder about Rowan's conversation with my parents until the following morning.

The clear cold from Christmas Eve was chased away by clouds that rolled in during the night. We woke to over six inches of snow on the ground with plump snowflakes still falling from the sky. My mother had gifted us a Christmas tree from a local artist who made decorative trees out of reclaimed crab pots. I pulled it out of the box, set it up on the table, and plugged in the lights just as Rowan came in from the bedroom. His hair was rumpled, and he looked sleepy. And *sooo* sexy.

"Good morning," I murmured as I crossed over and leaned up for a kiss.

He palmed my cheek, turning what I meant to be a brief kiss into a lingering one. I was flushed all over by the time he lifted his head. Sassafras bumped against our calves, and he peered down with a chuckle. "Well, good morning. She touches me now," Rowan offered as he looked back at me.

I laughed. "I know." I abruptly remembered my question last night and pressed my palm to his chest. "No more kisses until you tell me what you were talking about with my parents last night."

"Mae," he protested. "Can I please surprise you?"

"Fine, don't tell me," I muttered, turning and crossing into the kitchen. I was on the way to start coffee when he called my name.

When I turned back around, he was standing under the mistletoe that I'd jokingly hung a few nights ago. "What is it?" I asked. He looked rather serious.

"Well, you know…" Suddenly, he seemed nervous and shifted on his feet.

"Are you okay?" I crossed over to him.

He was wearing a pair of worn sweatpants. I was

partial to how they hung low on his hips because I could take a gander at his sculpted abs. He slipped his hand into the pocket, pulling something out. "All right, I won't wait," he said, almost to himself.

"Wait for what?"

He opened his palm, and my pulse rocketed. "Rowan? Is that what I think it is?"

He nodded slowly. "You said you loved opals, that it was your favorite stone. Remember?"

I blinked at the tears threatening to spill over. "Uh-huh," I whispered.

Years back, before we even went on our first actual date, Rowan had been present for a conversation in my dorm room. I didn't even remember which friend it was, but she was all giddy because she wanted to get engaged. That led to a conversation about rings, and I'd said my favorite stone was an opal even though it wasn't traditional.

"So, I talked to your parents about it last night. Not because I thought I needed anyone's permission, but because I know how much they mean to you. I'm trying to get things right this time. You know?"

I swallowed through the emotion thick in my throat, and a single tear slipped down my cheek.

"Mae, please don't cry. If this is too soon—"

"No, they're good tears," I said hurriedly.

Then he was stepping closer and sliding one arm around my waist. We looked down together at the simple ring he held in his hand. The iridescent opal shone under a ray of the early morning sun that broke through the clouds and fell in a hazy shaft through the windows.

"I can't believe you remembered that," I whispered.

"There's not much I forgot about you, Mae. I told

your parents that I loved you. I wanted them to know that, for me, you're the real deal. And, well, that's it." He took in a gulp of air.

"You're the real deal for me too. I'm sorry it took us so long."

"It's okay. You have nothing to apologize for. I'm just really glad I took the chance to come out here when I heard about the job. It was only ever us. You know that, right?"

It *was* only ever us. Then he was kissing me, and the ring fit perfectly.

I squealed and held it out for him. "I'm not the kind to freak out about jewelry, but it's pretty incredible you remembered that conversation."

His eyes were warm, and when he smiled, it felt as if a ray of the sun cast over my heart.

It was the best Christmas I'd ever had. After a relaxed morning, we went over to my parents for gifts and had lunch. All I wanted was time with Rowan. And that night in front of the fire, without the shag carpet, was everything I wanted.

Want a glimpse of the future for Rowan & Mae? Join my newsletter to receive an exclusive scene:

Sign up here: https://BookHip.com/QDGDJWW

p.s. If you are already subscribed, you'll still be able to access the scene.

Thank you for reading Rowan & Mae's story - I hope you loved it!

Up next in the Light My Fire Series is Archer &

Phoebe's story. Archer & Phoebe were childhood best friends until Archer moved away after fifth grade. It's safe to say they didn't have romance on the radar in those days.

Fast forward over a decade and Phoebe's ex cheated on her with her bestie. Archer is moving back to town and needs a wife. He offers to salvage Phoebe's pride. Before she can think twice, she's married to the man she used to jump in mud puddles with.

Archer's not supposed to be so tall, dark and damn sexy. They're supposed to be faking it. But there are definitely some things they are not faking.

Don't miss Archer & Phoebe's friends to lovers, marriage of convenience romance - it's hot, swoony and gooey sweet all in one!

Pre-order Fall For Me - due out Feb 22, 2022!

For more swoony romance...

This Crazy Love kicks off the Swoon Series - small town southern romance with enough heat to melt you! Jackson & Shay's story is epic - swoon-worthy & intensely emotional. Jackson just happens to be Shay's brother's best friend. He's also *seriously* easy on the eyes. Shay has a past, the kind of past she would most definitely like to forget. Past or not, Jackson is about to rock her world. Don't miss their story! Free on all retailers!

Burn For Me is a second chance romance for the ages. Sexy firefighters? Check. Rugged men? Check.

Wrapped up together? Check. Brave the fire in this hot, small-town romance. Amelia & Cade were high school sweethearts & then it all fell apart. When they cross paths again, it's epic - don't miss Cade's story!
Free on all retailers!

For more small town romance, take a visit to Last Frontier Lodge in Diamond Creek. A sexy, alpha SEAL meets his match with a brainy heroine in Take Me Home. Marley is all brains & Gage is all brawn. Sparks fly when their worlds collide. Don't miss Gage & Marley's story!
Free on all retailers!

If sports romance lights your spark, check out The Play. Liam is a British footballer who falls for Olivia, his doctor. A twist of forbidden heats up this swoon-worthy & laugh-out-loud romance. Don't miss Liam & Olivia's story.
Free on all retailers!

Light My Fire Series
    Wild With You
    Hold Me Now
    Only Ever Us
    Fall For Me - coming February 2022!
    Keep Me Close - coming July 2022!
Dare With Me Series
    Crash Into You
    Evers & Afters
    Come To Me
    Back To Us
    Take Me There - coming May 2022!
Swoon Series
    This Crazy Love
    Wait For Me
    Break My Fall
    Truly Madly Mine
    Still Go Crazy
    If We Dare
    Steal My Heart
Into The Fire Series
    Burn For Me
    Slow Burn
    Burn So Bad
    Hot Mess
    Burn So Good
    Sweet Fire
    Play With Fire
    Melt With You
    Burn For You
    Crash & Burn
    That Snowy Night
Brit Boys Sports Romance
    The Play
    Big Win

<u>Out Of Bounds</u>
<u>Play Me</u>
<u>Naughty Wish</u>
Diamond Creek Alaska Novels
<u>When Love Comes</u>
<u>Follow Love</u>
<u>Love Unbroken</u>
<u>Love Untamed</u>
<u>Tumble Into Love</u>
<u>Christmas Nights</u>
Last Frontier Lodge Novels
<u>Take Me Home</u>
<u>Love at Last</u>
<u>Just This Once</u>
<u>Falling Fast</u>
<u>Stay With Me</u>
<u>When We Fall</u>
<u>Hold Me Close</u>
<u>Crazy For You</u>
<u>Just Us</u>

RESOURCES

A note about Mae's story

Mae's story involves drug-facilitated sexual assault, an all too common crime on college campuses. It is estimated that between 19-27% of women will experience sexual assault in college and that approximately 47% of rapists are known to their victims (Rape, Abuse & Incest National Network, 2021). In addition, it is estimated that 68% of all sexual assaults are unreported (RAINN, 2021). Of those that are reported, 98% of perpetrators will never spend a day in jail (RAINN, 2021). For Mae's story and so many others, it is remarkably unrealistic for perpetrators to experience legal consequences. The emotional and psychological pain and shame that victims carry can be devastating. If you or anyone you know has experienced sexual assault, there are resources for help.

. . .

National   Sexual   Assault   Hotline: http://www.
thehotline.org
     1-656-4673 (HOPE)

National Sexual Assault Online Hotline: https://ohl.
rainn.org/online/
     Confidential online instant messaging and online
chat with trained professionals

National Dating Abuse Hotline (for teens and youth):
http://www.loveisrespect.org
     1-866-331-9474

National Center for Victims of Crime: www.victim-
sofcrime.org
     1-202-467-8700

ACKNOWLEDGMENTS

It's almost 2022, and it's been quite a ride in life and in my writing this past year. I remain so grateful for my readers. Thank you for loving my stories and characters.

My assistant, Erin, makes magic behind the scenes and helps keep me organized. My editor helped me whip Rowan & Mae's story into shape, and Terri D. swept up the details with her keen attention.

This gorgeous cover comes courtesy of Najla Qamber. In addition to an amazing eye and incredible design skills, she makes me laugh.

Huge thanks to my early readers who find any lingering mistakes, and to the bloggers who cheer on my books and so many others.

No book would be complete without the support of my husband, who gives me the time and space to write. Our dogs keep me company on my plotting jogs every morning. This was the first book I wrote with our new rescue puppy, so it meant lots of pee breaks for him. I'm happy to report he was potty trained by the end of the first draft.

xoxo

J.H. Croix

www.ingramcontent.com/pod-product-compliance
Lightning Source LLC
Chambersburg PA
CBHW070924190726
48292CB00004B/1089